R L
A Bello
x

Rosie baby!
Thank you so much
I really appreciate your
support!
love you
x

Order this book online at www.trafford.com
or email orders@trafford.com

Most Trafford titles are also available at major online book retailers.

Copyright © A.Bello 2012
Copyright © Cover illustration Giles Greenfield 2012

All rights reserved. No part of this publication may be reproduced, stored in a retrieval system, or transmitted, in any form or by any means, electronic, mechanical, photocopying, recording, or otherwise, without the written prior permission of the author.

Printed in the United States of America.

ISBN: 978-1-4669-1730-9 (sc)
ISBN: 978-1-4669-1732-3 (hc)
ISBN: 978-1-4669-1731-6 (e)

Library of Congress Control Number: 2012903496

Trafford rev. 08/10/2012

 www.trafford.com

North America & international
toll-free: 1 888 232 4444 (USA & Canada)
phone: 250 383 6864 ♦ fax: 812 355 4082

Acknowledgements

Big thank you to all my amazing friends, family and publishing team who supported me on this journey. Thank you to God for helping me to write this book and Dr Ramson Mumba for your amazing words of wisdom. To my brilliant A Team - Laura, Daniella, Lasharna, Arthur, Chelsea, Naomi, Frances and Giles. Thank you.

To Naomi
for everything

PROLOGUE

The Rogues

"Lox! Lox! Lox!" the crowd chanted, throwing their fists in the air and waving posters and banners.

Lox Knight was kneeling over, with his hands on his knees, breathing hard. He coughed violently, a tight feeling in his chest. His opponent was slowly stirring from the ground. It wasn't long before he would have to attack again. Lox wiped the sweat and dirt from his forehead. Something sticky trickled down his cheek. Lox wiped it off on the sleeve of his Dojo kit and looked at it. His blood shone vividly against the white linen.

"Come on, Son," a deep voice hollered behind him.

Lox stared into the dark eyes of his father, who was seated in the first row. He was dressed casually today, in jeans and a striped shirt with his trademark sunglasses. His 'disguise' he called it, even though everyone knew who he was. Lox thought it was a pathetic attempt at blending in and told his father so, many times.

Lox's opponent was slowly rising. His orange training kit was streaked with dirt, blood and sweat. It was torn at his torso, where Lox's fireball had hit. He was called Zeus, apparently after the Greek God because he truly did believe he was the best. This self-assurance and his huge power energy was the reason why Zeus was the three year running champion of the annual Warrior Tournament.

"Only a minute left to go. Can Lox Knight go the distance . . ."

The commentator's announcements were drowned out by the cries of Lox's loyal fans, chanting his name and blowing their horns.

"Lox! Lox! Lox!"

Here we go, Lox thought.

Lox closed his eyes. He could sense that Zeus's power energy had dropped significantly. Lox looked up at the clock below the commentators' box. Thirty seconds left.

He cupped his hands. His palms faced his opponent, who was shaky as he got up.

"Himyara, Himyara," Lox chanted.

He could feel the last of his energy draining out of his body, forming into a blue fireball, growing rapidly in capacity and power. The audience were cheering, his father was shouting but Lox was completely focused on Zeus.

Zeus was still shaky as he stood up to his enormous height. His head was spinning and his vision was blurred. He looked down at the little boy in front of him, focusing until his sight cleared.

"Who - who do you think you are?" Zeus said slowly as Lox smirked at him.

Dazed yet determined, Zeus charged, full speed towards Lox with his heavy fist raised.

Lox smiled, he loved this part. He watched as Zeus came closer.

"Now, Lox!" his father screamed.

But Lox waited. Only when Zeus's shadow hung over his small frame, did Lox holler "HIMYARA" and shoot his fireball with the last of his energy, hitting Zeus in the pit of his stomach. Zeus's eyes widened and his mouth formed a giant 'O' as the fireball threw him across the stadium,

I AM . . .

dropping him hard on the concrete floor, knocking him out. Some members of the audience buried their heads in their neighbours' chest while others cheered.

The referee raised the red flag and Lox punched the air in victory. The crowd hugged each other and applauded loudly and the paparazzi were pushing each other to get to Lox first. They were flashing lights and thrusting microphones into Lox's face.

Strong hands squeezed Lox's tired shoulders affectionately and he looked around to find his father was standing behind him, his brown eyes shining brightly as he looked at Lox. Lox tried to shake him off but couldn't.

"Tell me Lox, how does it feel to be the new champion?" a pretty, blonde reporter asked, shoving the microphone into his face.

"It feels good," Lox said.

"And being Thomas Knight's son must make it even more significant?"

"I don't see why it -"

"Thomas, Thomas how does it feel that your son is the new champion? Clearly inheriting your breathtaking skills that rid the world of Neci . . ."

It was happening again. Lox didn't know why they bothered. They only spoke to him to speak to his father. The press adored Thomas Knight. It wasn't because he, Lox had won because he was skilful and had trained up to the early hours of the morning, until his body ached and his Mum begged him to stop. No. They all thought it was because he was Thomas's son. Lox stepped backwards from Thomas. Thomas's hands slid off and he waved at his fans, who cheered and waved banners for him. The paparazzi closed in, circling Thomas until Lox could no longer see him.

The sky was a dull, dark grey. The streets were quiet. Everyone had gone inside fearing the thunderous rain they could sense was approaching.

No one saw Lox Knight walking along the deserted streets, enjoying the peaceful silence. His enormous rucksack kept hitting against his back. The rucksack was dragged down by its considerable weight.

He crossed the road, not bothering to look if any cars were coming. He tightened the straps of his bag so the straps dug into his shoulder blades. He smiled to himself. He liked the feeling of the bag pressed into his flesh.

The sky rapidly turned from grey to black and there was a sudden chill in the air. Lox shivered in his worn out, black hooded jumper and thin, black tracksuit bottoms. He took off his cap and pulled out the elastic band that was holding his ponytail, allowing his long black hair to fall over his ears, warming the sides of his face. No one was around so he pulled down the scarf that covered half of his face, hiding his identity.

He began to whistle tunelessly. He smiled at the familiar mansions. He was happy he wouldn't have to see them again. His phone vibrated in his pocket. A text from Dad. Lox deleted it.

No more training sessions with him or pretending that they were the perfect family. He wouldn't have to smile for the press anymore as Thomas rested his hands on his shoulders. Lox's victories would be his own and there would be no one to take them away.

"I'm free!" Lox shouted up to the sky.

Lox quickened his pace. He wanted to get to The Valley as soon as possible. He couldn't believe he had only heard about it a week ago from a girl at school, who had stayed there when she had family problems. It was a hidden underground spot where teenagers with powers could hide out. He would stay for a couple of nights until he thought of a better plan or before the other warriors ratted him out to the press for money. He would call his Mum in a few days to let her know he was okay. He hoped she would understand why he had to run.

I AM . . .

Lox stopped in the middle of the street and looked closely at the pavement. He pulled out a lighter from his pocket. A glow of amber rose from its top and he could now make out money on the pavement.

Lox hurried over and studied it. A twenty pound note. He laughed at his luck as he picked it up. Lox froze, he could hear quick footsteps behind him. He jumped back and dropped his lighter. He quickly wrapped his black scarf over his face and jammed his hat on his head. Lox reached into his other pocket for his knife which he held in front of him.

"Who's there? I'm armed," he said fiercely.

Silence. His voice sounded muffled through the scarf but as he looked around wildly, he couldn't see anyone. He could have sworn he had heard footsteps.

"Hello Lox," a woman's voice called from within the shadows.

Lox took a step back and held his knife out.

"Who are you?" he asked.

The woman breathed in the air deeply and sighed, "I can sense from you a great power. It's magnificent. Breathtaking."

Lox took another step back.

"What do you want?" Lox asked. The knife was shaking in his hand.

"You."

Lox felt his pocket for his lighter but it wasn't there. Baffled, he emptied both pockets, spilling loose money over the concrete floor until he remembered he had dropped it because of her.

"You want this?" the woman asked and floating in midair was Lox's lighter.

"How did you -"

"Take it," her voice cut in smoothly.

Lox hesitated. The lighter seemed to be coming closer towards him. He saw a glimpse of a white mask before the flame at the top shone bright in his eye. He jumped back and waved his knife around wildly.

"I swear if you come closer I'll -"

"Why have you got a knife child? When you can produce a fireball big enough to destroy this entire city? Or did you think I wouldn't recognise you with your face covered?"

Lox opened his mouth but was lost for words.

"I saw you at the Warrior Tournament a year ago. It's taken me this long to track you down but it was worth it."

She lowered her voice so that Lox moved closer towards her.

"You have an amazing ability. There is so much that I can teach you, there is so much that you must learn. I can help you."

Lox pulled down his scarf and stared at the woman coldly.

"I work alone."

He turned away from the woman to carry on with his journey but he stopped. He turned back around, facing her.

"Who are you?"

"My name is Rose Moore and I want to help you."

"Why?" Lox shouted, marching up to her. "Why does everyone want to control me? I didn't ask for your help! I don't need it!"

Rose laughed shrilly in Lox's shocked face.

"We are the same Lox," Rose said softly. "We're both warriors fighting alone. I know everything about you, Lox. I know everything about the warriors worth knowing. I know who you share blood with."

"Everyone knows he's my Dad," Lox said.

"Yes, they do," she answered. "But I know that he hasn't been there for you and your family, even though he promised he would be. I know that every time you defeat someone, he always gets the recognition and praise. I know you feel trapped by this man that you adore and despise. You're constantly torn between your love for him and the anger that rises inside of you every time you see him, testing your loyalty and freedom. I know deep down, you hate him."

Lox studied her black silhouette in silence.

I AM...

"You're so desperate for someone to notice you, Lox, and I do. Do not doubt what I can do for you," Rose whispered. "I'll make you invincible. A legend. Together, we will make history. Just take my hand."

Through the darkness, Lox saw her pale hand reach out to him, with vivid, scarlet scars etched all over them. Her long, black hair blended in with her black training kit, that hung tight on her lean physique.

"Take it and glory will be yours," Rose whispered.

The sky was an inky black. The rain drops felt light and refreshing. The sky was streaked with golden bolts. A second later, the rain fell heavily, soaking Lox's clothes until it stuck to his skin. His eyes didn't move from Rose's scarred hand.

"Glory would be mine?" Lox said.

Rose nodded, "You'll get all the praise you deserve."

"Would I be allowed to come back to see my family?"

"I was under the impression from your heaving rucksack that you wouldn't care to see them again," Rose replied.

Lox looked up and stared at Rose. Her dark eyes lit up as he put the knife in his pocket and seized Rose's battered hand.

"Let's go home," she said.

That was the last night that Lox Knight was seen in Legends Village.

Leah Knight cried in disbelief when she awoke the following morning, armed with pancakes and tea to find her baby. Gone. Everyday she stayed at home, just in case he came back, fighting the nightmare that he was lying dead somewhere. Lox's three year old sister, Emily, cried with her mother, unaware of the seriousness of the situation though she could sense her mother's sadness.

Three years later no one had heard a word.

Thirty-five million pounds was the going rate for his safe return. Thomas had left the family home years ago, promising Leah he would search the world if he had to, and would return home with their son.

The news blared everyday in their living room and newspaper articles were scattered over the marble floor bearing Lox's handsome face, as Leah waited for news on her boy or on Thomas, and yet nothing came. Every other day, somebody would call her confirming that they had spotted Lox somewhere and then ask for the reward money. Thomas returned months later, with no Lox.

A year later, Leah died from her long battle with breast cancer, leaving behind her seven year old daughter, Emily and husband, Thomas. A heartbroken Thomas, determined to fulfil his dead wife's last wish, went back on his search to find Lox. He moved Emily's godparents, Sally and Michael Meran into his family mansion and they became Emily's legal guardians. As Emily got older, her father visited less and less until the visits stopped altogether.

CHAPTER ONE

The Osaki Training School

Emily Knight touched the bird shaped necklace on the display. She picked it up and held it to her neck. She thought the contrast of the blue against her caramel skin was beautiful. Emily looked around the shop. The staff were running up and down the stairs, there was a long queue at the till and the burly security guard was talking to a lady pushing a pram.

Emily slipped the necklace into her jeans pocket. She continued to look at the other displays, gradually filling up her pockets with jewellery.

"Excuse me but you're banned from this shop."

Emily recognised the chubby, blonde lady, today wearing a pink, knitted dress who was frowning at her. She had caught Emily shoplifting twice. Some of the customers, stopped and stared. One of them pulled out their camera phone. Emily shrugged her shoulders.

"Am I? Cool. I'll leave."

Emily turned to go but the lady grabbed her arm tight.

"Hey!" Emily clenched her fists.

"Aren't you forgetting something? That jewellery hasn't been paid for."

"I ain't got nothing," Emily spat, unclenching her fists and a small fire flame flickered in the middle of it. "So take your fat hands off me."

The lady released her when she saw the flame.

"Right. Ahmed," she called over to the security guard, who winked at the woman with the pram.

He marched over to Emily, shouting codes into his walkie talkie.

"Be careful she's one of the them," the lady whispered to the security guard.

"One of what?" Emily said angrily, as the flame turned red.

"Do you want to empty your pockets Miss?"

"Like I told her," Emily said, through gritted teeth. "I ain't got nothing."

The security guard raised his eyebrows and pointed at her pocket. A flower pendent was hanging out of it. Emily's flame rapidly disappeared.

"Let's go downstairs," the blonde lady said, when she saw the customers staring. "I believe you know the way."

She stared coldly at Emily, who rolled her eyes and allowed herself to be led towards the stairs.

Emily placed her forehead on the wooden table, listening to the clock tick by. A policeman next to her tutted and shuffled some papers, beside her. Emily looked up and saw him reading the newspaper. The headline read KNIGHT'S FREE SPREE IN HARRODS and underneath was a picture of her, holding Harrods shopping bags and six security guards chasing after her. Emily snickered. The policeman looked at her and turned the paper over so he could see the headline.

"Stealing isn't funny. It's a serious offence."

"So I've been told. That's the good thing about being rich, you can buy your way out of anything."

The policeman put down the paper and looked sternly at Emily.

"Why didn't you pay for the jewellery or the things from Harrods? It would be petty change to you."

Emily stared at her nails, checking to see if her nail polish was ruined, "Didn't feel like it."

The policeman picked up his paper.

I AM . . .

"Spoilt brat," he muttered.

Emily hit the front of the paper so that it fell out of the policeman's hand.

"I don't care what you or anyone thinks!"

"When I get a hold of that girl!"

Emily and the policeman watched as the office door opened and a skinny, scraggy faced woman with long, oily, brown hair and small, grey eyes stormed into the room.

"You!" Sally Meran screamed at Emily, who looked unfazed. "How many times do the police have to keep calling me over you stealing? If your father could see you -"

"Well he doesn't," Emily cut in, rolling her thick black hair into a messy bun. "They've got back all the jewellery so can we go?"

"Do you even know how wrong stealing is?" Sally asked, walking towards her.

"I've heard it's pretty bad," Emily said, smiling at Sally.

"Don't you be smart with me young lady," Sally snapped.

"Ms, she was caught with £200 worth of jewellery," the policeman informed Sally, who's mouth dropped open.

"Which is nothing to the thousands I almost got from Harrods," Emily added in.

"Enough!" Sally roared, pointing at Emily. "Just be quiet!"

Emily sighed and placed her head back on the table as she listened to Sally apologising to the policeman. Emily hated getting caught. Always the same lecture. Sally saying she doesn't know what to do with her, then her husband, Michael complaining that they were letting Thomas down and they had to be stricter on Emily. Then Jenny Li, her counsellor was called and Emily had to talk to her about her issues.

Emily didn't feel she had issues. She knew she was an angry girl but who wouldn't be? Her mother had died, her brother had run away causing her father to go and chase after him so she had no family around her. Sally and Michael were her godparents but also fostered a whole bunch of kids who lived with them in her family mansion. They loved that Emily was a warrior and constantly hassled her to show off her powers. They thought she was cool because she was the daughter of Thomas Knight, the leader of the Five Warriors. The five greatest warriors to exist; Thomas Knight, Roberta Taniana, Hubert Jenkins, Cecil Archinia and Niles Thompson.

They built their reputation on defeating evil warriors, using their powers for good, saving lives and winning world wide warrior competitions. They were treated like rock stars by warriors and non-warriors. Boys loved Roberta Taniana because she was beautiful and strong and girls loved Niles Thompson because he was sixteen and gorgeous but Thomas became the most popular amongst everyone. He was the only warrior in the world to battle the evil Neci and win.

Neci was notorious for winning battles and killing her opponents. Her aim was to be the strongest warrior in the world and she didn't care who she had to kill to succeed. She had famously killed Cecil Archinia and Niles Thompson in the same battle that Thomas had won. The deaths of Cecil and Niles eventually ended the heart broken Five Warriors. After her first loss, she had fled. No one knew where and no one hoped to see her again. Thomas had gone down in History for being one of the greatest warriors that had ever lived.

Emily always thought of the day when she had got her powers. She was seven. She had ran crying into Sally and Michael's room, screaming as smoke surrounded her hands. She felt like her flesh was burning off. Michael had grabbed the bottle of water by his bedside table and threw it at Emily. The water sizzled as it hit her hands and the smoke disappeared. Sally grabbed Emily's hands, she turned them over and looked at them astonished, as her hands were fine.

I AM...

After that night, Emily had felt different. She felt stronger, faster, her senses were heightened, her body felt lighter. She wasn't surprised by the changes to her body or even that they came years earlier than the average age (warriors usually received powers when they turned thirteen). Lox and Thomas's powers had also come early. But she didn't expect her powers to come and go as they pleased. One minute she could barge through walls, making them crash down around her, then the next minute she would knock herself out as she charged at the wall and it stayed solid.

Emily hated that she was constantly compared to Thomas and Lox. She hated that she had no control over her powers. She hated that the kids at school treated her differently out of fear or adoration.

Sally refused to send Emily to private school like the other warrior kids on their street. Instead Emily was sent to public school to keep her more grounded but Emily stood out like a sore thumb. She was harassed with questions about her family, money, even about her famous neighbours to the point where Emily asked Sally to fire the driver and maids and to get rid of the Aston Martin just so she could fit in a little bit more. But what Emily really hated the most was everyone assuming that she was this brilliant, skilful warrior and she wasn't.

It didn't help that she lived in Legends Village. An exclusive neighbourhood where the residents were either famous warriors or families of famous warriors. Everyone lived in five storey mansions with an indoor swimming pool, cinema, training room and a zillion bedrooms. She was surrounded by excellence. She lived next door to Roberta and Hubert Jenkins from the Five Warriors, so the press camped in Legends Village. They would be outside her door waiting for a story, hoping that they had found the next 'legend' in her.

One time she was taking the younger foster kids to the park and they were immediately ambushed by the press. Bright lights flashed at them and the kids had started to cry. Emily had felt an anger rise up in her and before she knew it, most of the paparazzi were on the floor, knocked out. The kids were screaming and Emily rushed them all into the house. She didn't know what she had done and how she had done it but since then she had had a reputation as a dangerous brat.

"Emily, Emily!"

"Huh?" Emily said sitting up and rubbing her eyes.

"Come on, we're going home," Sally said before she marched out of the office.

The car ride home was quiet. Emily kept glancing at Sally, waiting for her to explode but Sally remained tight lipped. Emily took out her mp3 and put the headphones in her ear. Before she pressed play, Sally rested a hand on her leg.

"Yeah?" Emily asked, removing the headphones.

"I was so worried that you had sent more security guards and paparazzi to the hospital. I've run out of 'Get well soon' cards."

Sally's mouth twitched as she looked at Emily.

"I did have a flame but I got rid of it. You know I don't mean to hurt them. I don't even know how I do -"

"I know," Sally interrupted, squeezing Emily's leg gently. "But we have to fix this Emily. You can't go through life hurting people and hoping they'll understand. You need control. There are already people out there who are scared of warriors and make it harder for you to exist and adding thieving on top of it, doesn't help. You don't want your Dad reading in the paper how his daughter is stealing from Harrods! When you have millions in the bank. He'll start thinking Michael and I are pulling the wool over his eyes."

Sally laughed to herself but Emily didn't reply. She hoped that her father would see her in the paper and rush home, when he saw his thieving daughter as front page news. It was her way of telling him that she needed him. She stared down at her hands as if they would give her the answers to her dilemma.

I AM . . .

"But we will fix this Emily, that's a promise," Sally said as she turned the car on to their street, filled with rows of mansions with perfectly kept gardens.

Emily nodded and put back in her headphones.

There was a quiet knock on the door.

"Come in," Emily called from her desk.

She closed the text book she was reading and Michael Meran popped his head around the door and pushed up his squared glasses.

"Hey Ems, you busy?"

Emily shook her head. She noticed he was wearing the grey checked shirt she had got him for his birthday. He didn't know it was stolen.

"I was just doing some summer homework."

"Oh good, good. Do you mind coming downstairs quickly?"

Emily got up and followed Michael down the stairs.

"Am I in trouble?"

"No, honey," Michael said, looking back at her and smiling. "I think you're going to really like this."

Michael led her into the grand dining hall where Sally and Jenny Li were sitting around the oak table. It was the only room in the house not covered with toys and hair products.

"Hi, Emily," Jenny said excitedly.

Jenny was a pretty Chinese woman, with shoulder length auburn hair. She was wearing a short, white summer dress that showed an ample amount of her toned thigh. In contrast to Sally, who had her oily hair tied up into a messy ponytail and was wearing black leggings and one of Michael's faded University of Kent jumpers.

Jenny patted the seat next to her and Emily sat. Emily leaned on the table but it was still sticky from when her foster sister, Rosy had spilt her juice at dinner. At times like this, Emily missed the maid. Emily kept her hands in her lap.

"So what's going on?"

Emily looked at the three of them.

"Well Emily, we've reviewed your file with Jenny and we all felt it was important that we found you the right type of support," Sally said.

Emily frowned, "Support?"

"With your powers," Michael explained. "We know that when warriors are thirteen, they receive their powers and are meant to join a training school. We know you got your powers early but they're developing quickly, probably too quickly and we need to find a way to keep them under control."

"So now that you're thirteen, we've found this," Jenny said, sliding over a prospectus.

Emily picked it up, staring at the colourful cover. It had a picture of two young warriors sparring over a beautiful koi pond.

"The Osaki Training School?"

"Oh Emily, it's brilliant," Jenny said, pointing at various pictures on the prospectus. "They teach Martial Arts, they have Meditation rooms, they even teach you how to breathe under water!"

"Really?" Emily asked dubiously, re-checking the information.

"Yes! And so many famous warriors have come from there. Tainwo Kena, Penelope Summers, you know, she was the youngest warrior ever to play Dojo professionally," Jenny said knowingly.

"And don't forget the Five Warriors," Michael chipped in. "Roberta Taniana, Jenkins, Cecil and Niles."

"Your father," Sally said.

"My Dad went here?"

Sally nodded, "The Five Warriors formed at this school. It's where they all discovered their amazing powers. Emily this could be you."

Emily laughed, "I dunno about amazing power but if they can help me control it, that would be great. So when does it start?"

"It starts September 3rd. It works just like a regular school. You go in from Monday to Friday. You can get a bus from St Bertudes, which would take an hour. Driving is forty minutes or to fly is twenty but then it depends how fast you can fly. You can't fly can you?" Jenny asked.

Emily shook her head.

"I think she'll get driven," Sally said sternly, looking at Emily.

"You already have a place because you're a Knight so all we need to do is get your training kits and you're all set so what do you think?" Jenny said it all in one breath.

"Well," Emily said slowly. "I think it sounds . . . okay."

"Just okay?" Jenny said astonished. "Emily I know you're not in love with your powers but this is first class training! There is the option of staying up there, would you prefer that so you can be with your friends?"

"I haven't made them yet!" Emily said, rolling her eyes. "And no, I don't want to be stuck in a room with some weird girls. I'll just commute."

"Emily, are you okay?" Sally asked frowning. "You don't sound too pleased."

"Look, it's bad enough being at a school where everyone treats me differently. Now I'm going to go to this school where they worship my Dad even more and people will just be expecting too much from me."

"Emily, this is a fantastic experience and who cares what anyone else thinks about you? You just do the best you can do as you've always done," Michael said, smiling at her. "We all want what's best for you. You do know that?"

Emily nodded and looked around the table.

"Thank you, I do appreciate all your effort," she said. "I just need some time to get my head round this. I'm going to take this upstairs and read through it."

Emily left the table, hugging the prospectus tight to her chest. When she opened the door to her room, she was instantly bombarded with questions.

"So, what was it?"

"What's happening?"

"Are you leaving?"

"You're smiling - why?"

"Guys!" Emily shouted over the racket the kids were making. She hid the prospectus behind her back. "I will tell you all in the morning. Now go to bed, it's way past your bed time."

"Oh," James Evernham, Rosy Lang-Sheen and Yvonne Saunders moaned.

"But you're going to tell Cathy, aren't you?" Rosy asked, crossing her arms and pouting.

Cathy Lee shook her head solemnly, making her blonde curls bounce, "I promise, I'll find out in the morning too."

Cathy crossed her two fingers at Rosy. Clearly satisfied, Rosy skipped out of the room hand in hand with Yvonne.

"Emily, Emily!" James said, running up to her. "You know tomorrow can we play 'Smash the Bricks' in the garden? I want to see if you can break them all with just one punch."

Emily laughed, "Sure but I think I smashed them all from the last game."

"Oh." James looked crestfallen. His brown fringe fell into his eyes.

"I'm sure Dad will buy some more," Cathy said, making James jump up and down.

"Yeah, he will. I'm going to ask him now," James said, running out of the room.

Emily made sure he had gone all the way downstairs before she hopped on to her bed and placed the prospectus on the bed.

"Wow, what is this?" Cathy grabbed the prospectus. "Osaki Training School. You're going to a training school? Oh my gosh!"

I AM . . .

"Yeah," Emily said miserably.

"Don't get too excited," Cathy said as she flicked through the prospectus.

"I admit it does sound cool but they're just going to treat me the same aren't they?"

"You don't know that," Cathy said, putting an arm around her. "Look, if this is as good as it looks then I'm sure it'll be worth the hassle. Emily, this is not about them. This is about you. For safety reasons you need to get this under control."

Emily smiled, "So there will be no more walls falling down . . . by accident anyway."

Cathy laughed. "Exactly. Mum and Dad would be grateful that you're not destroying this gorgeous house. I wonder what they're going to think when they see you? It's Emily Knight, daughter of the sexy Thomas Knight, the thirteen year old Harrods thief."

"Shut up," Emily laughed, throwing her pillow at Cathy, which missed and hit the wall. "And please don't call my Dad sexy, that's weird."

Cathy laughed.

"I still can't get over you stealing from Harrods," Cathy said, running a hand through her curls, as she stared in awe at Emily.

"You dared me to," Emily said defensively.

"I know but I didn't think you would. Emily," Cathy moved closer to her. "This whole stealing phase isn't really funny anymore. I mean, Harrods was crazy! I know you said your Dad will only remember you if you're on the cover of every paper but I doubt he's forgotten you, how could he?"

Emily sighed and fell back on to the bed, with her arms under her head, "Well I've been in the papers religiously for about two years with no contact so I need a new plan anyway. Hey! Maybe when they teach me how to fly, I can fly all over the world to find my Dad."

"As long as you take me with you," Cathy said. "We'll leave a note for Mum and Dad."

Cathy stretched out her arms and yawned, "I guess that's my cue. See you in the morning babe."

"Night Cath," Emily said as Cathy left the room.

Emily got up and paced around her large room. She stared at her four poster bed, the family pictures on her bedside table and back to her bed where the prospectus was. Emily picked it up and left her bedroom. She walked down the hallway and opened the last door. She put on the light and looked at Lox's bedroom.

It had not changed since he left as Thomas wanted to keep it the same for him for when he came back. He had pictures of battles everywhere, on his bed covers and the walls. All of his trophies were lined up in his glass trophy case. There was a massive picture of him holding the Warrior Tournament trophy with their father, right behind him. Emily always found Lox's expression odd in that particular picture because he was smiling but there was a sadness in his eyes.

Emily always visited Lox's room whenever she was uncertain of things. She wasn't sure why but she felt like she could think better in his room. Emily sat on his bed and re-opened the prospectus, she read through the first paragraph before she felt the energy level. It felt like someone was watching her. Emily eyes darted from left to right, the presence was getting stronger. Emily closed her eyes. The energy level was very strong and was coming from the window. The wind was blowing Lox's curtains up and Emily grabbed them and wrenched them open.

She gasped when she saw a person, floating in front of her, covered head to toe in black, so all Emily could see were light brown eyes. Emily could make out a lean, muscular figure, with prominent biceps. The pair locked eyes and neither of them moved or spoke. Emily opened her mouth but words seemed to escape her.

"Don't go," he said in a deep voice.

"W-What?" Emily frowned.

I AM . . .

"Don't go there," he said, before he slowly started to fade away until he was gone.

Emily stuck her head out of the window, searching for the person but he had disappeared. She closed her eyes, she couldn't sense his energy either.

"Don't go where?" Emily shouted but she had no response.

CHAPTER TWO

Warside

"Emily, is that you?"

Emily walked into the kitchen, holding the Osaki prospectus in her hand. Sally was covered in flour and a horrible smell was coming from the oven. Emily pulled a face and covered her nose with her hand.

"What's up?" Emily asked in a muffled voice.

"Please, please, go and keep an eye on the kids. They're in the indoor pool. I don't know where Cathy is."

"Okay, sure."

Emily headed towards the pool. James was doing a canon ball into the water and Rosy and Yvonne were playing mermaids. Emily sat at the edge of the pool, with her feet in the water. She opened the prospectus and flicked through it. Emily squealed when she felt something wet drip on to her arm.

"Watch it James!" Emily said, wiping at her wet sleeve.

James was hovering over her, reading the prospectus.

"That sounds so cool."

Emily looked at the prospectus. It was on breathing under water.

"It sounds like committing suicide," Emily said, turning the page aggressively.

"I wish I could go to this school," James said wistfully, as he sat beside her.

Emily scoffed, "I wish I didn't have too."

"Why?" James asked, as he stared at her with his huge green eyes.

"Because I'm going to be surrounded by my Dad's obsessive fans that's why."

James stayed silent. He put his feet in the water and watched them float.

"All I know is, if I had a chance to learn half the stuff you're going to, I wouldn't care about how everyone else acted towards me. My progress would be the important thing."

Emily looked at James and she couldn't help but smile.

"When did you get so wise?"

James looked at her, "I learnt from you."

And before Emily could digest the impact of his words, James was already on his feet and he dived gracefully into the pool.

Emily had read through the Osaki Training School prospectus four times before Jenny arrived to take her to Warside. She had to admit, the school sounded incredible; the lessons she was going to learn, the people she was going to meet. She was intrigued to see what she would be able to do with her powers.

Jenny arrived that afternoon. They were driving to Sia's Avenue, a half an hour away from Emily's house, where their nearest Warside was. Emily couldn't see any press outside the house but never the less, she ran into the car wearing a baseball cap hung low, covering her face and she quickly shut the door.

"Beautiful day, isn't it?" Jenny said, as she admired the late August sunshine.

"Mmm," Emily said, as she read the prospectus once again. "Did you know you can only inherit your powers? It says here that it's possible for powers to skip a generation and turn up again years later.'

Emily closed the book and looked at Jenny. "That means your Granddaughter from the year 2035 could be the first to get powers since your Great Grandma. Ain't that weird?"

Jenny laughed. She glanced at Emily's face.

"It's nice to see you happy, Emily. So you're excited now about the school?"

Emily frowned, "Hmmm more curious than excited."

They arrived at Sia's Avenue earlier than they had planned. It was covered in cobbled roads and was full of fancy restaurants and vintage shops. It was the sort of place Sally refused to take her shopping as everything was overpriced and she had to clothes shop for five children. Emily wished she could shop there but she didn't have access to her savings until she turned eighteen.

Emily saw Warside first. It was a huge, white building with karate kits, displayed on the burly models in the window. When the two entered the store, they were surprised to see it overcrowded with school children and their frantic parents. The sales assistants were running back and forth from the changing rooms, holding heaps of karate kits in their arms; their white t-shirts damp from agitation.

Emily touched a white karate kit, and was studying it with interest, when a young, spotty, ginger haired boy approached them, smiling broadly at Emily. She jumped back surprised and Jenny giggled nervously.

"Hi, I'm Donny. What can I help you with today?" he said in a surprisingly deep voice.

Jenny placed her hands securely on Emily's shoulders and squeezed them lightly.

"She's starting the Osaki Training School this term and she needs a uniform and a training kit, please."

Donny nodded his head attentively, "Size?"

"Ten," Emily replied, looking over Donny's shoulder.

Two attractive boys around the same age as her, were looking at Emily curiously. One had floppy blonde hair and high cheekbones and the other was mixed race, with big hazel eyes and was wearing a blue cap. They were whispering and pointing at her. Emily pulled her hat down lower.

"Emily!" Jenny called.

"What?" Emily said, looking away from the boys.

Jenny and Donny were already walking away from her. She glanced back at the boys but they were gone. Donny led them to the far end of the store. He handed Emily a white training kit in her size.

"These are training kits. They're similar to karate kits but they're much lighter so you're not weighed down when you fly. This is your uniform."

He handed her a dark blue training kit. Emily held it up. It felt light, with long sleeves and had big gold buttons running down from the collar to the bottom, along the middle of it. Each button had the letter 'O' inscribed. The bottoms were baggy, blue trousers that reminded Emily of pyjamas.

"I like this," Emily smiled.

"Thank God," Jenny muttered, under her breath.

Jenny glanced around the store and spotted a crucial piece of Emily's uniform.

"I'm going to check out the baht shoes for you, yeah," Jenny said, walking off.

"The what shoes?" Emily called but Jenny was too far to hear.

The changing rooms were spacious. Each one was designed differently. Emily entered the one with a picture of two warriors firing a fireball simultaneously at each other over a sandy pitch. Emily hung up her new training kits and stared at them. She removed her hat and tried on the school uniform first. She cringed at her reflection. The uniform was shapeless and hid her small frame.

"This is terrible!" she cried.

"You can say that again," a female voice said from the changing room beside hers. "I look like an idiot."

Emily giggled. She tugged at the sleeves, which were hanging past her hands. She rolled them up but groaned at her reflection.

"This really isn't working," Emily muttered to herself.

The girl from the changing room next to hers laughed, "I'll show you mine if you show me yours?"

"You're on," Emily replied.

She stepped out of the changing room and turned to face a pretty black girl, with long black braids and big brown eyes who was staring back at her.

"What are you on about?" the girl said. "You look fine!"

"So do you," Emily replied. "The mirrors are not our friends!"

The girl laughed. They both turned to look in the giant mirror in front of them and in the reflection, Emily watched as the girl squinted, frowned and murmured to herself.

"You look really familiar? Have we met before?"

Emily rolled up her sleeves again, whilst avoiding the girls gaze.

"I don't think so."

Emily walked back towards her changing room, praying that she wouldn't be recognised. The girl's eyes followed her but she didn't say anything.

When she was dressed back in her skirt, white vest top and her baseball cap pulled down low, Emily opened the curtain to her changing room to find the girl standing in front of her. Emily jumped and dropped her new training kits on the floor. The girl hurriedly bent down to pick up the items.

"I'm so sorry for scaring you," the girl gushed.

"It's okay, don't worry," Emily said quickly.

I AM . . .

"No I just-"

"It's okay-"

"But I think-"

"It's fine!" Emily said assertively. She breathed in, then calmly said. "It doesn't matter."

She took her training kits from the girl and held them tight to her chest.

"You're a bit touchy for an overrated celebrity," the girl said, watching Emily carefully.

"I'm not an overrated celebrity," Emily replied.

"Says the girl who's famous for being Thomas Knight's daughter, stealing from Harrods and not being able to control her powers?" the girl replied swiftly.

Emily looked around the changing rooms. They were alone. She removed her cap and shook her dark, thick hair out.

"I knew you looked familiar," the girl said, winking at her.

"Please don't tell anyone," Emily begged. "I just want to shop in peace."

The girl smiled at her and held out her small hand, "My name's Michella Kinkle and yes before you ask, I am Janette Kinkle's sister."

Emily shook her hand and looked at her confused, "Emily Knight. Who's Janette Kinkle?"

Michella gave an exaggerated gasp, "You don't know who . . . but you must, I mean . . . oh!" she said, slapping herself on the forehead. "Are you a Manchester Fountains fan?"

"A fan of what?"

Before Michella could answer, Jenny walked into the changing room. She was holding a pair of what looked like, black ballet shoes with a thick grip at the bottom.

"Any luck?" she asked Emily.

"I need a smaller size in the training kits. What are those?" she pointed at the shoes Jenny was holding.

"Baht shoes."

"So you're going to Osaki? Maybe we'll be in the same classes," Michella said.

"Yeah, maybe," Emily replied.

Emily handed Jenny the training kits. Jenny placed them over her shoulder. She smiled politely at Michella, who smiled back.

"Ready to go?" Jenny asked.

Emily nodded.

"See you later," she said to Michella.

"Bye! Nice to meet you, Emily. See you at school!" Michella waved.

After a long, loud and heated 'discussion' about the baht shoes in which Emily said she wouldn't be caught dead in them, because they were hideous, they finally made it to the check out.

"So, were my eyes deceiving me or did you just make a new friend?"

The words 'overrated celebrity' buzzed in Emily's head, words that she had read about herself in the papers. But when Michella had said it, for some bizarre reason, it didn't sound horrible.

"Yeah," Emily said laughing. "I think I did make a new friend."

The summer holiday rushed by in a blur. Emily had resigned from St Mary's Secondary School to the celebration of all the teachers except for Miss Keen, her Australian English teacher who thought Emily was a hoot.

Emily knew the Osaki Training School prospectus off by heart. She had read every book she owned on warriors (staring at her father's picture that graced most of the covers) so she had a better understanding of the sort of powers she would possess.

I AM . . .

Emily awoke at nine am sharp. She pulled on her school uniform and winced at her reflection. The uniform was still shapeless but it fit better than the last. She left her bag in the hallway and took a seat at the dining table, where porridge was being served. Emily played with her food and her heart leapt every minute the clock ticked.

"You okay?" Sally asked Emily, as she peered at her over her cup of coffee.

Emily nodded. She glanced at the clock. It was quarter to nine.

"Why do I even have to go in today? Lessons start tomorrow," Emily asked.

"Because today is the induction and where you find out what team you're in. Now, hurry up and eat," Sally said.

Emily rolled her eyes and continued to play with her food. The other children were quietly eating their porridge. James could barely hold his head up.

"Why are you guys up so early? You don't start school today?" Emily asked.

"Mum made us so we could see you off on your first day," Cathy spat. "And it's not even a proper school day for you. I'm so bloody tired."

"Where's Michael?" Emily looked at the vacant chair.

"He had to go into the office early. I know he was meant to drive you up but Jenny should be here soon to take you to school."

The door bell rang. Emily bolted to the door, with Rosy and Yvonne running behind her. She breathed deeply and opened it. It was Mrs Maynard, the maid from next door. She was still dressed in her pink housecoat and slippers.

"Morning!" Mrs Maynard called brightly. "Is Sally in my love? I was wondering if I could borrow some sugar 'cause Mr Peila can't take no tea without any sugar."

"Yeah sure," Emily said. "I'll just grab some for you."

The children ran back to the dining room. Emily went into the kitchen and poured sugar into a bowl and gave it to Mrs Maynard.

"Thanks my love," Mrs Maynard said.

Emily sat back in her chair, when the doorbell went again. She opened it and Roberta Taniana was at her doorstep. Her elbow length black hair was tousled around her pale, heart shaped face. Her large, almond, green eyes were enhanced by the black eyeliner that was swept seductively over her lids. She smiled kindly at Emily, showing off her white, shining teeth and her famous beauty spot on the right of her full, pink lips. She was tall and graceful, yet still curvaceous and sexy. Emily was always struck by her beauty.

"Aunt Roberta, what are you doing here?"

"I just wanted to wish you good luck on your first day," Roberta said, clapping her hands excitedly.

"It's only the induction today."

"Oh I remember how nervous I was when I opened my envelope. It's very important what team you're in Emily. They'll be like your family but you're an Ogragon girl through and through."

She gave Emily a big hug, "You must be so excited."

"Yeah, ecstatic," Emily mumbled into Roberta's ample cleavage.

"I'm dropping the boys off at school so shall I take you to Osaki?" Roberta asked, smiling at Emily.

"No!" Emily said and Roberta frowned.

"I mean, Jenny's already taking me so it's all good."

The last thing that Emily wanted was Roberta causing a media frenzy when all Emily wanted to do was blend in.

"I'll call round soon and let you know how it's going. Say hi to Uncle Jenkins for me."

"Okay, honey. Bye."

Emily closed the door and sat on the stairs, biting her nails. She watched anxiously as the cars raced past the house. One stopped. Emily heard the engine switch off and watched Jenny come closer to the door. The doorbell rang. It was ten o' clock. Emily didn't move. Cathy hurried out of the dining room and glanced at Emily.

"Lazy cow!" Cathy spat bitterly.

Cathy opened the door and Jenny stood there holding two cups of hot chocolate.

"Hi," she sang as she came into the house.

Cathy grunted in response and walked back into the dining room.

"What's wrong with her?" Jenny asked.

"She's tired. So are we going?"

"Yep, go and grab your coat. I've got your bag."

Emily ran into the front room and grabbed her coat from the armchair. Sally rose from her seat and followed Emily into the hallway with the children behind her.

"Bye Emily," her foster sister, Rosy, called from the front door.

"I'll see you guys this evening," Emily said.

"Make sure you find the hotties!" Cathy called and Emily laughed in response.

Emily walked up to Sally and hugged her. She couldn't remember a time when Sally had hugged her so tight. Sally ruffled Emily's hair affectionately which she knew Emily hated. Emily swatted her hand away and smoothed it back down. She waved once more at her family before she entered the black car with Jenny already sitting in the front seat.

"Nervous?" Jenny asked, handing Emily a hot chocolate.

"Yeah," Emily whispered truthfully. Jenny grabbed her hand and squeezed it gently.

The car roared to life and Emily looked back, waving furiously at her family. They drove in silence until Jenny's phone vibrated. She quickly checked it and muttered, "Oh crap," before she turned the car around.

"What's wrong?" Emily asked.

"Sorry babes, got an emergency counselling session. You'll have to get the bus."

"The bus!" Emily squeaked.

"Yes the bus. Are you too posh to get the bus?" Jenny teased.

"No but . . . what if there's some out of control kid who blows up the bus?"

Jenny glanced at her and then burst out laughing, "Honey, I think that's what the kids will think when they see you!"

"Do you think so?" Emily asked, feeling anxious. "What if they're all scared of me? What if I do blow up the bus?"

"Emily I was joking! You'll be fine. Breathe child."

As Emily took deep breaths to calm herself before she had a complete meltdown, Jenny explained to her that she was taking her to St Bertudes Bus Station where all of the Osaki students would meet to get the coach up to the school.

They arrived at St Bertudes half an hour later. They had only walked a short while, when Jenny and Emily stopped and stared. The station was full of coaches and buses. Thousands of them, in different colours and sizes.

Jenny led her to a row of dark blue, huge coaches and she looked at her watch.

"The coaches are due to leave in ten minutes, so make sure you get a good seat. Sally or Michael will collect you from the school this evening."

A tear fell down Jenny's cheek.

"Jen why are you crying?" Emily asked, as she wiped at her wet cheeks.

"Ignore me," Jenny said. She pulled out a tissue from her pocket and blew into it violently. "I'm just so proud of you."

Emily laughed, "Your nose is red."

Jenny rolled her eyes and wiped at it, which only made it worse. Emily hugged Jenny tight around her waist. They clung to each other for a while, neither of them saying a word. People walked past and stared at them but they didn't move.

"Don't be afraid to be you. Don't live up to anyone's expectations but your own," Jenny said.

She kissed Emily softly on the forehead, hugged her once more, and walked off.

Emily stood alone and watched Jenny disappear. She took a deep breath and climbed on to the coach. It was noisy, loud and packed. Most of the seats were occupied but Emily found two vacant seats next to each other.

Emily sat on her seat and gazed out of the window. She saw Michella, hurrying to the coach with her family. She had a lot of siblings. Emily watched them as they embraced each other.

The engine of the coach started and everyone who was not on the coach gave hurried kisses to their loved ones and ran to the coach. Emily's stomach was in knots. Someone flopped on to the seat beside her. It was Michella.

"Thanks for saving me a seat," she said smiling.

"Err . . . your welcome," Emily said uncertainly. "You alright?"

Michella nodded her head, "Just the usual. My Mum giving us a lecture to be good little kids but I think that was aimed at Warren. He's been suspended twice."

"Oh, why?"

Michella sighed, "He just gets at the teachers, d'you know what I mean? He doesn't listen to anyone, he constantly breaks the rules. Then he drags Pete - my other brother - with him, and Pete's pretty cool when he's not around Warren."

"So how many people are there in your family?"

"Four brothers and two sisters," Michella said, taking off her jacket. "I'm the fifth one to join the school. But the eldest, Janette has already left."

"It's quite nice having a big family," Emily said.

Michella looked at her and pulled a face.

"No way! They're all so talented, it's ridiculous. Janette, Lenny, Warren and Pete are all athletic, really good in battles," Michella said ticking them off her fingers. "Then Mike is amazing at music, drama and dance and Madison is a child model. Then there's me."

Michella sighed.

"What are you good at?" Emily asked gently.

Michella shrugged her shoulders, "Nothing really. I would say I'm the smart one because I'm rubbish in battles, can't sing, dance or act to save my life and I'm not that pretty -"

"You are," Emily interrupted.

Michella smiled, "Thanks but compared to Madison, I'm just average. I know I'm smart but Lenny gets better grades than me so I guess I'm just an average warrior with average powers but I wish I was more than that."

"You might have hidden powers. You never know."

Michella laughed, "Yeah, maybe. I love my family but they're so annoying, so I'm very glad I'm staying at the school. Anyway enough about me, tell me all about your family. I know you live with your godparents?"

Emily nodded, "Yeah, they're pretty cool. I'm the eldest. My godparents foster kids so I've got three foster sisters and one foster brother."

"Oh. I heard about your real brother."

"Yeah?" Emily said, looking out the window. They were on the main road.

"Lox, right? And he ran away?"

Emily nodded, "I was only little when it happened."

Michella frowned, "My mum told me he ruled the Warrior Tournaments. He was like a little Thomas Knight. Seems to me he had it made, so why would he do that?"

I AM...

Emily frowned, a question that she asked herself constantly, "I don't know."

"You must see the other Five Warriors all the time? Obviously not Cecil and Niles 'cause there dead. I still can't believe that. I'm so glad Thomas finally got Neci for that," Michella said.

"Yeah Aunt Roberta and Uncle Jenkins live on my road. We live in Legends Village."

"Whoa," Michella said. "I don't know why I'm surprised, you're obviously minted."

Emily laughed uncomfortably. She racked her brain to take the topic away from money.

"Did you know Cecil and Niles rejected going to Par Bliss? Aunt Roberta told me," Emily said.

"No!" Michella gasped. "I thought Par Bliss was a myth? Why would you reject Warrior Heaven?"

"I'm not sure. Aunt Roberta said that warriors are blessed with these abilities and if they use them for good, when they die they have a choice. To stay in Par Bliss or keep doing good on earth," Emily explained.

"Wow, give up Heaven. I mean it's Heaven!" Michella said. "Maybe because their lives were taken from them, they felt like they had more to give?"

"Yeah, maybe."

There was an awkward silence. Michella glanced nervously at Emily.

"So . . . do you know how to do fireballs and fly already?"

Emily laughed, "Only by accident! Didn't you read the story about me knocking out all the paparazzi outside my door?"

Michella laughed, "Yeah I remember that, oh I'm so glad. I thought you were going to be some protégée or something. I only know a bit because my older sister, Janette plays for the London Flyaways so she taught me some moves."

Michella pulled out a packet of sweets from her pocket and held it out to Emily.

"Macnocs Liquorice?"

"Thanks," Emily said taking one. "I've never played Dojo before and I've only seen a couple of matches. Our TV's constantly tuned into the kid's channels. What are the rules?"

It took Michella a while to explain the eight players and what they had to do to win the match. There were usually five Fighters and three Distracters in every team. Michella's sister Janette, was a Distracter.

"See Janette is perfect for her position 'cause she's covered in tattoos, right? And she has this massive one on her back -"

"Yeah, I remember that one," a voice said above them.

Emily and Michella looked up and Emily immediately recognised the boys from Warside. They were leaning over Emily and Michella's seats and they stared at Emily with interest.

"Hey, these are my friends. We grew up together," Michella told Emily.

"This is Emily Knight. *The* Emily Knight," Michella said to the boys.

Emily waved, feeling slightly embarrassed.

"Hi, I'm Jason Notting."

The blonde haired boy smiled at Emily. He was extremely handsome, with prominent cheekbones and deep blue eyes.

"And I'm Wesley Parker. I knew it was you at Warside."

He had light brown, curly hair and was wearing the same blue baseball cap from the store. He stared at Emily with his intense hazel eyes so that she had to turn away.

After an hour of laughing, talking and playing a game of cards, the sky was now shining brightly above them. They were now in a valley of fields. Emily's stomach rumbled loudly. Michella, Wesley and Jason looked at her and laughed.

I AM . . .

"Your turn, Wesley," Michella said.

Wesley looked at the pile of cards before he put down two black jacks. Jason swore loudly, making them all laugh. He hesitantly picked up eight cards.

"No, mate. You're missing two!" Wesley said gleefully.

"I picked up ten!" Jason argued.

"Liar," Emily said smiling.

"Michella, do you remember at the party after his Bar Mitzvah and Jason somehow had all the Black Jacks? You're a rubbish cheat Jas," Wesley said, nudging him playfully.

Michella threw two cards at Jason. He threw his cards angrily at the floor and marched away from them. Emily clutched her stomach and laughed loudly.

"Are we here?" Wesley asked, as he pointed to a giant building up ahead.

"Hey, there it is!" a girl called from the back of the coach.

"Wow, look at those mountains," the boy in front of Emily said.

"Mountains?" Emily said. She looked out the window and gasped when she saw them in the distance.

Eager children pressed their faces against the cold glass as the coach travelled up a long, upwards slope. It came to a halt outside a tall, white, five floored building covered in elaborate patterns constructed out of gold. The first floor had a huge black slanted roof with 'The Osaki Training School' in bold, gold letters. Each floor was built on the previous floor's roof and each floor got smaller and smaller. It reminded Emily of the Russian dolls Yvonne played with, where you open one up and the doll inside it is smaller. There was also a long walkway that was attached to the ground floor walls that went in opposite directions. Emily saw a few adults, who she assumed were teachers walking across it. Emily's nose hurt from being pressed against the window. She pulled her face away and rubbed it.

"Wow," she whispered, looking at the building in awe, not believing that this was her new school.

"I feel like I'm in a manga," Wesley said, as he looked up at it.

Several people had began to take down their suitcases. Michella and Emily looked at each other and together, they pulled down Michella's heavy suitcase.

"Where's yours?" Michella asked.

"I'm commuting," Emily said, as she stepped on to the grassy floor.

Hundreds of students were vacating the coaches. Emily stayed close to Michella. Her palms were sweating and she couldn't stop looking around.

"Look," Michella whispered.

Emily turned her head and watched as the two wide front doors began to open.

CHAPTER THREE

The Six Teams

The students fell silent as a short, Chinese man in a cream coloured training kit with slick black hair walked through the front doors.

"I'm glad to see you have all arrived safely," he said softly. "Could all the students except for the first years, please take their belongings into the hallway and take a seat in the dining hall."

Emily jumped out of the way as the students hurried past her, laughing and talking loudly. A girl with cornrows bumped into Emily. Emily instantly clenched her fists but the girl turned around and apologised and Emily unclenched her fists feeling ashamed. She watched them enter a door on the left.

"Hello first years. My name is Laton Chin," he smiled at them. "I am the deputy headmaster and I welcome you all to the Osaki Training School. As you may have noticed, the buildings are on top of one another. This is traditional Japanese architecture and each building is a different department. Let's begin with a tour of the school."

Everyone began to talk excitedly and grabbed their suitcases. Emily followed the students through the front door and into a spacious hallway. It had wooden floors and the walls were white with inscriptions along them.

"Love, peace, faith," Emily read aloud one of the inscriptions.

Michella grabbed Emily's arm, making her stop, "Look."

This particular wall had quotes from famous warriors and Michella was pointing at one from Emily's father.

"Having powers is a blessing and using them for good is the biggest honour, quoted by Thomas Knight from Super Flight Magazine 1998," Emily read.

"That is so cool," Michella said. "I'm going to see who else they've quoted."

Michella ran off ahead and Emily re-read the inscription until she knew it of by heart.

"In the first year you will learn the foundations of warrior history and controlling your powers," Laton Chin said. "You will take History lessons, Water Studies, Flying, Martial Arts and Meditation. Let's go to the Meditation room first."

Laton Chin led them to the end of the hallway, where there was a set of oak doors. He opened them to reveal a striking pond, surrounded by colourful flowers and exotic plants.

"Oh wow," Emily said, as she looked into the pond and saw bright fishes darting too and fro amongst the rocks and petals that had fallen from the trees.

"This is the koi pond. I know it looks lovely so please avoid jumping into it," Laton Chin said. "As you can see all the fields over there lead on to the forest, where our deer reside. You are allowed in the forest but please do be careful to not scare the animals. Follow me this way."

Emily watched Laton Chin walk over a curved bridge that went over the koi pond. There was a huge tree with pretty pink flowers, that hung over the bridge. The branches were low enough to pick one of the flowers. It was beautiful. The bridge led to a wooden patio area.

"Isn't this amazing?" Michella squealed.

I AM . . .

"It really is," Emily said.

She heard a clicking noise behind her and saw Jason taking pictures of Wesley, who was posing in the shots. Emily laughed.

"Guys you're going to see this every day."

Wesley took the camera off Jason and looked at it, "It's not for me, it's for my Mum. She's never been here before 'cause she's not a warrior but she'd love all this."

"Oh, can't families come up to visit?" Emily asked, as Wesley passed her the camera. She flicked through the photos. He looked cute in them.

"Maybe but she can't because she's in rehab."

Emily gasped, "Oh . . . why?"

"She's an alcoholic," Wesley said, casually.

"Oh," Emily said again, surprised at Wesley's casualness.

Jason grabbed the camera from her. She looked over at him but he was taking pictures of the fishes. Emily opened her mouth and closed it. Wesley looked at her amused.

"Emily it's cool, you don't have to say anything."

"Okay," Emily said relieved. "I didn't know whether to say sorry -"

"Why would you say sorry?" Wesley asked, smiling. "You didn't make my Mum a drunk."

"No, I know," Emily said blushing. "It's just . . . I dunno I thought that was the right thing to say . . . sorry, I'm just blabbering on."

Wesley touched her arm gently, "Don't worry, like I said it's fine."

He smiled at her once more and walked off ahead.

"Jason," Emily called.

"Coming," he called back. He took one last picture and hurried to join her.

They caught up with the rest of the first years who were standing on the patio. The patio led to an open spaced beige coloured room where the floors were covered with blue mats. There was a giant window on the other side that faced the koi pond.

"You will notice that there is minimal furniture in the school especially the classrooms. This helps in being able to focus on what's intended and a clutter free space makes it easier to clear the mind. Let's move on to the Foughtgon room," Laton Chin said.

The Foughtgon room, where they would learn Martial Arts was in the basement of the school. It was a gigantic, cream coloured room with inky black scriptures written on the walls, in a language Emily couldn't recognise. Like the Meditation room, there were blue mats that covered the floor.

On the second floor was the Water Studies room. Emily instantly disliked it. It was a room with a big see through tank in the middle of it. It looked bland compared to the other rooms she had seen.

"This is how we learn how to breathe under water?" Emily loudly asked. "It looks like a giant fish tank."

"Well in the second year, you get to practise in the river in the forest," Laton Chin said to her. "And the reason why we have a see through tank is so we can make sure our students are not drowning."

"Oh," Emily blushed. She noticed that a lot of the students were staring at her and nudging each other. When Laton Chin said they were going up a floor to see the History class, Emily followed straight after him.

"Oh, why did I have to open my big mouth?" Emily sighed. "Now they all know I'm here."

"But they would find out sooner or later," Jason said, as they walked up the stairs.

"Yeah but the latter would have been better."

The History class wasn't impressive either. It had a triangular roof and six rows of chairs with a giant blackboard in the middle. The only good thing was it had a giant window which faced the impressive fields.

"Something to do when we're bored," Emily whispered to Michella, who looked at the window and laughed.

I AM . . .

Flying lessons were in the school stadium. Emily chose to admire it from the stands so she wouldn't get sand in her shoes. The stadium was a circular shape with at least a thousand red seats. There were huge circular lights that shone on to the pitch. Above the red seats was a smaller booth which was for the commentators. The scoreboard underneath the commentators' booth read, 'Dojo Champions - Pentwon.'

"Hi."

Emily, Michella, Jason and Wesley turned around and saw a group of girls smiling broadly.

"Are you Emily Knight?" a girl with red, short hair and a spotty face asked.

"Guilty," Emily sang.

"I knew it!" a black girl with curly hair said. "Didn't I say? Didn't I?"

"Okay Ola," a brown haired girl said sharply and Ola was instantly quiet. "So Emily, do you have any special powers at all?"

Emily shook her head, "Not that I know of."

"Oh," the girl said, looking disappointed. "But you can fly and teleport already can't you?"

"No," Emily said again.

The girl frowned at Emily, "I don't get it. There's nothing really special about you is there?"

Everyone fell silent. Michella put her hands on her hips and raised her eyebrows.

"Err," Emily said. "That's why I'm here to learn. Sorry I didn't catch your name."

"I didn't offer it," the girl sneered before she walked away with her army behind her.

"Who the hell was that?" Emily asked. She watched the brown haired girl walk on to the pitch.

"I don't know but she was rude!" Michella said, kissing her teeth. "I do not like her."

"Forget her," Wesley said, pointing to the pitch. "Laton Chin's calling us over."

They hurried over to the crowd that had formed around Laton Chin. He was smiling at them.

"I hope you are satisfied with the school. There are still many places to discover but to show you all would spoil your fun. Before I dismiss you, I must place you in a team. The teams will be like your family. You will battle with them, train, meditate and grow with them.

"There are six teams at Osaki, named after the six leaders of the Warrior Revolution, Idris Jenkint, Bernard Ogragon, Rose-Marie Mentorawth, Joseph Berbinin, Arthur Linktie and Ce-Ce Pentwon. If you are the first in your family to receive powers and we couldn't trace your family history, you have been placed randomly in a team but if we could trace your family, then you're in the same team as your family would have been. So let's begin."

Twenty six students emerged on to the stadium, wearing t-shirts with giant letters on them and carrying boxes.

"It is easier to track everyone when you know what team they are in. You'll progress more in a smaller group and if you want to play Dojo, you'll play for your team," Laton Chin explained. "Now, in an orderly fashion, can everyone please line up in front of the person bearing the first letter of your surname and collect your envelope."

Michella grabbed Emily's hand and dragged her to the girl, with streaked red hair, chewing gum with a 'K' on her top. A Korean boy with long black hair in a long braid stood in front of Emily. They smiled at each other. Emily nervously pushed her hair off her face.

"Name?" the girl asked in a bored voice.

"M. Kinkle," Michella said.

The girl handed her an envelope.

"Name?" she asked the boy.

"J. Kena," he said.

When he got his envelope, he opened it and smiled to himself. Emily caught his eye.

"What team are you in?" Emily asked, hoping that she sounded causal and not intrusive.

"I'm in Mentorawth," he said.

"Name?" the girl asked Emily.

"E. Knight," Emily said.

"As in Emily Knight? Thomas Knight's your Dad?" the red head asked, with the first sign of animation Emily had seen.

"Yep that's me."

"Cool!" the girl grinned. She frowned as she rummaged around in the box and Emily began to panic.

"Here you go," the girl said. She handed her an envelope.

Relieved, Emily took it. She watched Michella open hers very slowly and then grin like a Cheshire cat.

"Ogragon, my brothers are in that. Well open yours."

Emily opened her envelope. Her heart was pounding in her ears.

Ogragon or Mentorath, Ogragon or Mentorawth. Emily pulled out the small piece of paper, which was neatly folded in the middle and she smiled.

"Ogragon."

Michella squealed excitedly and hugged a surprised Emily. Over Michella's shoulder, she watched J. Kena walk silently away.

"You are all dismissed. You can either go to your rooms or relax in your team living room and meet your fellow team members. Lunch will be served in half an hour in the dining room. Anyone not staying is free to leave after lunch. If for any reason you need to stay overnight at the school then please inform your team leader. Lessons will start tomorrow and you will meet the headmaster at breakfast. Now go and enjoy yourselves," Laton Chin said.

The students applauded him and he bowed his head to them. There was instant chatter and the students began to walk in different directions.

"Hey!" Emily called out to Wesley and Jason as they walked towards her and Michella. "We're team Ogragon. What are you two?"

"Ogragon," they said simultaneously.

"That's perfect," Emily squealed, hugging them both. "What shall we do first?"

"I want to check out the rest of the school to take more pictures for my Mum," Wesley said.

"Yeah, I'll come with you," Jason said to him. "We'll meet you two at lunch."

They walked off, with their bulging rucksacks on their backs, getting a few admiring glances from the first year girls.

"Living room?" Michella asked.

"Definitely," Emily said.

They walked up to the school doors. Emily couldn't help but look around as she went, taking in the scenery. A crowd of students ran down the steps towards them causing Emily and Michella to jump out of the way.

"We're walking here!" Emily shouted after them.

"Jeez what's the big hurry?" Michella asked, picking up the suitcase she had dropped.

"Hey Mich," a tall boy with the same almond eyes as Michella, called out.

"Hi, Warren. I got into Ogragon."

"Of course you did," he said, giving her a high five. He looked down at Emily with his hand outstretched. "Warren Kinkle, Michella's loving brother."

Emily laughed as she noticed the mischievous gleam in Warren's eyes, "Emily Knight. Nice to meet you." She shook his hand.

"You stole from Harrods in the summer right?"

Emily shook her head, "Nah, I got caught."

Warren laughed, "Better luck next time. The most outrageous thing I've done is getting the teachers to reach their mid life crisis a few years too quick. Clearly I need some tips."

"Really? I've heard you're a bit of a trouble -"

"Okay," Michella cut in, looking at them both sternly. "Let's not encourage each other shall we? Warren be useful, where's the Ogragon room?"

Warren scratched his bushy hair, "Oh, up two floors, then take a right. You can't miss it, it says Ogragon in big letters. Catch you later."

He bent his knees and flew up into the air and out of the door.

Michella cupped her hands around her mouth, "I'm sure you're not allowed to fly!"

Warren turned around mid-air, "I'm sure if I cared, I wouldn't be."

He zoomed off. The first years watched him in awe. Michella rolled her eyes, "D'you see what I mean about him?"

Emily looked back and could faintly see Warren near the stadium, "He seems like a laugh to me."

Michella scoffed and walked off ahead, leading the way.

Laton Chin was right, the school was very spacious. The only type of clutter was on the walls. There were quotes everywhere and giant paintings off Dojo matches, that would take up an entire wall. On the second floor, Emily got distracted by a wall that had hundreds off pictures on it. It was called the 'Osaki Wall of Fame.'

"Michella, check this out."

"Huh?" Michella said, walking back towards Emily. "Wow, I didn't even see it. Look, there's my sister!"

Michella pointed to a lean girl who held a red fireball in her hand. She had long, straight, silky black hair and a cute button nose. One of the sleeves of her Dojo kit was torn, exposing a tattoo with three fairies, holding hands.

"That's cute," Emily said, pointing it out.

"Yeah, it's meant to be me, her and Madison. She's covered in tattoos."

"Janette Kinkle, Distracter for London Fly Aways and England Dojo Team," Emily read of the plaque. "Wow impressive."

Michella sighed, "Yes it is."

"Look, there's Tainwo Kena. He was in one of the warrior books I read," Emily said. "He created light beams. The fireballs that can blind you for up to an hour. Hey, do you think his related to that J. Kena?"

"Who?" Michella frowned.

"Remember he was in front of me to get our envelopes. Long black hair, really cute . . ."

Michella continued to look at her blankly.

"Never mind," Emily blushed. Michella raised her eyebrows at her.

They continued to search the wall. Michella found the Five Warriors first. Emily was transfixed by the picture. They were posing in the middle of a stadium, with an army of fans behind them. The eldest, Cecil Archinia, a short, blonde haired man; the beautiful, curvaceous, Roberta Taniana. Hubert Jenkins stood very tall and handsome with a protective arm around Roberta, making a breathtaking couple. Niles Thompson, the youngest, stood awkwardly at the side, smiling shyly, revealing cute dimples and lastly Thomas Knight, the leader was in the middle. Emily looked at his kind eyes and winning smile, wishing she could see them for real.

Michella whistled, "That's a long list of achievements."

"Yes it is," Emily agreed, tearing her eyes away from her father. A picture next to theirs, caught Emily's eye and she gasped when she saw it.

I AM . . .

"What?" Michella said, looking over at her shoulder.

"It's Lox, my brother. Oh my gosh."

It was a picture taken in the middle of a battle. Lox was crouched over to the side, with his hands by his chest holding a blue fireball. His muscles were bulging and he had a deep frown line in his forehead.

"Lox Knight, the youngest World Warrior Champion and Warrior Tournament Champion."

Emily couldn't help but wonder if she would ever join her family on this wall. She looked at Michella, "You see, we've both got big shoes to fill."

Michella smiled at her, "Yeah but I feel better knowing yours are so much bigger." She nudged Emily playfully, who stuck her tongue out at her, "Let's go find our room."

They found their team room with ease. Behind the door was a large living room. There were cream armchairs, bean bags and a huge mahogany table with small coffee tables scattered around. A red haired woman was hovering halfway in the air and placing a photo frame above one of the chairs.

"Hi," she said cheerfully, when she saw Emily and Michella. "I'm Ms Macay, the team leader of Ogragon."

She touched the ground and shook both their hands.

"Michella Kinkle," Michella said.

"Emily Knight."

"Ah another Kinkle and a Knight. Lovely. What did you think of the tour?" Ms Macay asked, as she pushed her glasses up her nose. Emily noticed she had pretty, green eyes.

"This place is amazing!" Emily said.

"I can't wait to start training," Michella said.

"Yes, that's what I like to see, enthusiastic students! Well I'm glad you girls like the school and I see you have your suitcase. Are you not staying, Emily?"

Emily shook her head.

"Well that's a shame. Girls if you go through there, Michella can pop her suitcase in the bedroom."

Emily and Michella waved goodbye to Ms Macay and walked to the bedroom. The bedroom was a sunny shade of yellow with 'LOVE' inscribed into one of the walls. There were eight double beds, pine wardrobes, a full length mirror and a huge window which faced the school stadium. They were greeted enthusiastically by the girls in their room, who instantly rounded on Emily.

"I'm Lisa Fowler," a petite girl with a blonde bob said. "I just have to say your Dad is absolutely amazing. Honestly I don't care what anyone else says, I am his number one fan and I have this massive poster of him over my bed with his shirt off. Oops, sorry you probably didn't what to know that."

"Oh my gosh, I can't believe you're on our team," Sydney John said, shaking out her long hair. "I've got to tell my Mum 'cause we've got a celebrity in OUR team! How many people can really say that?"

"We can!" Nicky Johansen said, nudging Sarah John so hard that Sarah's glasses fell on the floor.

"But your Dad is totally fit!" Violet Hijen said. "And your brother's dead cute too."

"I was so in love with Lox," Lisa said, placing her hands on her heart. "I hope he's found soon so I can marry him. Then I can be your sister!"

"Oh . . . okay," Emily said awkwardly as Michella laughed at her.

"I'm Daisy Atam," another blonde girl said, with two pigtails in her hair. "What do you think of the school?"

"Yeah it's ama -"

"I'm sorry Daisy is it?" Sarah John asked. "You have Emily Knight in your room, who cares what she thinks of the school? She robbed Harrods!"

"Oh my gosh you did!" Sydney John said, looking impressed.

"What did you take?" Nicky Johansen asked.

And all through it, Emily smiled politely not getting a word in as the girls talked and squabbled over each other and Michella and Daisy unpacked their belongings, clearly uninterested in the excitement of Emily Knight.

"So, how was it?" Sally asked, as Emily walked towards the car.

"It was good. The school's really impressive."

"And did anyone make a big deal about you?" Sally asked.

Emily laughed as she thought about the girls on her team, "A few but it was okay."

"I'm making a pie for dinner," Sally said. They both got into the car.

"Oh gosh Sally, don't make me be off school with food poisoning!"

"Ha ha," Sally said.

She turned on the engine and drove off. Emily looked back up at the school and smiled. She silently wished that she didn't have to leave at all.

CHAPTER FOUR

Cecil and Niles

The Ogragons had been seated in their first lesson of the year for over an hour, gossiping amongst themselves. They were in History with Mr King, who was hidden behind a fashion magazine. His worn out black shoes were propped on top of his desk. He hadn't yet addressed his class.

Michella was frowning deeply at Mr King as Danny June was boasting that he was related to Pearl June, a famous actress.

"Yeah, more like famous in the seventies," blonde haired Lisa Fowler scoffed.

"Fame is fame," Danny said, combing his afro. "You won't be cussing when I'm chillin' in Legends Village."

"Yeah, well me and Jason are personal friends with Janette Kinkle," Wesley boasted. "*And* she's Michella's sister."

"Shut up!" Danny said in disbelief. He dropped his afro pick.

"It's true," Jason said, flicking his fringe to the side as the Ogragon girls watched him adoringly. "Innit, Mich?"

Michella's eyes were still transfixed on Mr King. Jason nudged her and Michella looked at her peers distractedly.

"What? Oh, yeah. She's my sister - Emily?"

Michella nudged a sleeping Emily, forcing her to wake up.

I AM...

"Yeah," Emily said lazily, stretching out her body. She hadn't slept well last night so had overslept that morning and was late to school but seeing as the teacher didn't seem interested in teaching, she was catching up on much needed sleep.

"Why has our history teacher not moved from that same position since we got here?"

"Maybe he's tired," Emily said, closing her eyes.

But she was finding it hard to fall back asleep with Michella hissing in her ear.

" . . . But it's like what the headmaster said at breakfast, you know about absorbing everything you can? But how can I? When he just sits there! I mean, what's the point of paying to come to an institution of learning when your own teacher can't even be bothered! I don't blame you for sleeping."

"So why won't you let me?" Emily said, gritting her teeth. "If you've got such a problem with it, then tell him."

"I will," Michella said, standing up. "Mr King?"

Mr King did not respond. The class fall silent as they watched Mr King turn a page in his magazine.

"Mr King?" Michella asked concerned. "Sir, is everything okay?"

From behind the fashion magazine came a dramatic sigh. Mr King, a pale man with a long nose wearing a beige bowler hat, stared at Michella with disinterested eyes.

"And you are?" he drawled.

"I'm Michella Kinkle, sir. Err . . . I was just wondering why we -"

"Kinkle?" Mr King said sharply, interrupting her. "Warren, Pete - mean anything to you?"

"Yes, they're my brothers, sir," Michella said defensively.

Emily noticed how Mr King's eyes narrowed dangerously. She tugged at Michella's school uniform.

"Maybe you should sit down," Emily whispered but Mr King had already gotten up. His long frame towered over Michella.

"Do you know what your brothers did to me, Miss Kinkle?" Mr King said, throwing his fashion magazine on the floor and walking slowly towards a nervous Michella, who shook her head.

"Anyone? Anyone have any idea what her demonic brothers did to me?" Mr King said, looking wildly around the room at nervous faces.

"This!" he yelled theatrically.

He took off his beige bowler hat to reveal a bald head, with a few, threadlike strands of hair. Michella covered her mouth in horror as a huge gasp echoed around the room. Mr King watched their expression change and nodded his head.

"That's right, this was the work of your brothers," he cried, pointing at Michella. "All of those years trying to teach them. They sucked all the joy out of me. They stressed me to a point of no return. My fiancée left me!"

Mr King grabbed Michella by her shoulders with a desperate look in his face.

"I don't care anymore. I don't care about this job, about you, about anyone. Do you hear me?"

He let go of Michella and looked at his class, seemingly oblivious to the fact that they had huddled together at the back of the room.

"I'm still getting paid by the hour and when you all fail your exam - which you will! I will be sunning it up in Rio carnival and you can all blame her mother for giving birth to evil!"

Mr King turned on his heel and marched out of the door, slamming it behind him. The class sat in stunned silence.

Wesley giggled nervously, "Well, that was . . . erm . . . scary."

"You can say that again," Sydney John said, with her hand on her chest.

Michella was rooted to the spot, her face frozen in terror. Emily stood up to put her arm around her shoulders.

I AM . . .

"You okay?" Emily asked concerned.

"He said . . ." Michella began, her bottom lip trembling. "He said . . ."

"I know, it was well out of order calling your brothers evil," Emily said.

"No, not that," Michella said turning to Emily, her face in complete horror. "He said, he said we're going to fail the exams. If I fail the exams, that makes me worse than average. I'll be a failure!"

And with that, Michella burst into loud, noisy tears and flung herself on to a shocked Emily, who held her tight.

After an hour later of Michella sobbing, it was time for their next lesson of the day. Foughtgon Class with Berbinin.

They walked down to the basement of the school and entered a set of cream coloured doors. Even though they had already seen it, they still stopped and gazed in amazement. The blue mats were piled in a corner and there was a row of buckets containing glistening water at the back of the room.

"This room's really something!" Jason said, looking around.

The entrance doors opened and Berbinin trooped in, also admiring the room. Emily looked excitedly to see if J. Kena was there but was disappointed when she remembered he was in Mentorawth.

"This is gonna be interesting," Wesley whispered in Emily's ear but before Emily had the chance to ask him why, she heard cheers around the room. Emily turned and stared at the centre of the room where a small, old, Japanese man was standing, but he looked transparent.

"Oh, wow," Emily whispered, when she realised that every second that passed, the old man was looking clearer and clearer until eventually, he was standing in the middle of the room, rock solid.

"What did he do?" Emily asked Michella.

"He teleported. Isn't that cool?"

The old man put his hands together and bowed to them all.

"When I bow to you, you bow back. It's a sign of respect," he said in a soft voice.

Emily followed the lead of her class, who bowed back to the man.

"Sit, sit," he said.

After he gestured to everyone to sit on the floor, he joined them, sitting cross-legged. The old man pointed at himself, "I am Master Zen. Welcome to Foughtgon class. In this class, you will learn techniques on how to battle an opponent using Martial Arts and how to transform the energy inside you to create fireballs. But most importantly, you will learn how to control the power that you have now and how to build on that - yes?"

"Will we learn how to teleport?" a boy from Berbinin asked, putting his hand down.

The students grew excited and began to talk at once. Master Zen put a wrinkled finger to his lips until the class fell silent.

"I'm afraid that won't be for another two years."

The class groaned and Master Zen smiled, "The same response every year. Now, as you look around the room, you will notice that it is somewhat empty, so we have enough space to battle. The walls are made out of Masonka, an amazing material that absorbs the power that is given to it and in turn the walls become stronger, so no matter how powerful you are, the walls will not break. Over there at the back of the room in the buckets is Reviving Water. What is Reviving Water?"

Jason put his hand up. Master Zen nodded at him.

"In Britain, it can only be found in Mount Senai and it's water that when drunk, revives the person's energy level to its maximum power."

"That is good," Master Zen said.

"How did he know that?" Emily whispered to Wesley.

"Jason's annoyingly smart. You'll notice soon enough," Wesley said.

"The writing on the walls around the room is in Hariem. It has been here since the school was formed two hundred years ago and it is rumoured that it contains instructions on powerful fireball techniques. So if any of you are fortunate enough to read in the ancient Hariem, you can learn the secrets from the founders. There is no one in the school, that we know of, that can speak Hariem," Master Zen said.

He looked around the room and smiled at them, "I have two special guests who are going to help you with your battling skills. Every year for the first years' first lesson they come and teach. They have made warrior history with all the good deeds they have done with their powers and they have won the World Warrior Tournament countless times but you have to promise me that you will be different from the other years and not scream, shout and jump at them, okay?"

The class nodded. Emily did too, even though she had no idea who it could be.

"Okay gentleman, you may come in now!"

Two silver figures in training kits floated through the Masonka walls. One was a short, old, round man with a silver beard and round-shaped glasses while the other was a tall, comely teenager.

"OH MY GOSH! IT'S CECIL AND NILES!" Nicky Johansen screamed.

The class erupted in screams and excited shouts and everyone ran towards them. Master Zen rolled his eyes and the ghosts of Cecil and Niles laughed at the excited class.

"You're my fave warrior!" a girl in Berbinin shouted at Cecil.

"Niles, I love you!" Violet Hijen screamed.

"Marry me, Niles!" Lisa Fowler shouted.

"He's dead, you idiot!" a boy from Berbinin responded.

The commotion didn't stop until Master Zen intervened and shouted at them to sit down and button up.

"I can't believe they're here," Emily whispered to Michella. "We were just talking about them yesterday."

"My family never told me they were here. This is amazing," Michella squealed as she hugged Emily. "I mean it's Cecil and Niles!"

Cecil laughed at the overexcited teenagers and Emily knew that if Niles had blood pumping through his veins, his face would have been red.

"It's lovely to meet you all," Cecil said, smiling. "I'm Cecil Archinia and this is Niles Thompson. We're here to talk about what it takes to be a fully-trained warrior."

Some of the students clapped at Cecil's introduction. Wesley clapped the loudest, looking at them in awe.

"Skill is important when you're a warrior," Cecil said, scratching his bald head. "Training is vital as you never know what situation you may find yourselves in, so you must always be on top of your game. When the Five Warriors were around, we trained everyday for at least six hours, sparring and meditating with one another, encouraging each other to be stronger. What would you say is the most important skill, Niles?"

The young ghost of Niles Thompson frowned in concentration. A group of girls beside Emily looked longingly at him.

"I would have to say it's acceptance. I don't know about you guys but I first got my powers when I was seven years old. It's true," Niles added when he saw the shock on their faces. "I hated my powers. I didn't tell my parents for a whole year that I had them 'cause I felt so weird. But then I met Thomas Knight at a warrior competition."

Most of the students glanced at Emily who purposely kept her eyes to the front.

"And he made me realise that it was a blessing and not a curse. There are so many warriors who use their powers for evil. They use it to scare, intimidate and kill others. They abuse the gift given to them. You're all

I AM...

here because you've been blessed with this gift." Niles looked around the room at all the new students.

"Everyone should aim to use their gift for good. We are one family. We should be working together and be courageous enough to stand up to those who abuse their powers. Warriors and non warriors have lived in peace together for so long now. Neci tried to ruin that for her own selfish gain. It's our responsibility to keep the peace.

"We can save lives with our gifts. There are warriors who work in hospitals because they have healing powers and are helping sick people every day. That's why were here. It's why the Five Warriors even existed. We had to train and control our powers so we could get a better understanding of ourselves and protect innocent people."

"Well said Niles," Cecil said, smiling at him. "Can any of you sympathise with how Niles felt?"

Emily put her hand up as well as Wesley, Jason and some other pupils. Cecil and Niles looked at them all but their eyes lingered a second longer on Emily.

"After I met Thomas, I began to train with him," Niles continued. "And I started to understand my powers. I came to this school and I continued to grow. I had so many special gifts inside of me, it was amazing to see it all come out. Thomas, Roberta and Jenkins were in their forth year when Thomas formed the Five Warriors. Cecil had already left school but he and Thomas were good friends and he was also asked to join."

Jason put his hand up.

"Yes?" Niles asked.

"What kind of special gifts can a warrior get?"

"There are so many my boy," Cecil said, stroking his beard. "Fire breathing, healing, visions, weather control, telepathy - but sometimes it can just be unlimited strength. The list is endless but Niles here has telepathy, I have healing powers, Roberta has visions, Jenkins is an illusionist and Thomas has unlimited strength."

"Wait, you still have powers even though you're dead?" Wesley shouted aloud.

"And why did you reject Par Bliss?" Michella shouted out after.

"One question at a time," Master Zen said to Wesley and Michella, who fell silent.

Niles frowned, "Let's put it this way, we have powers but we can't physically hurt people. We can make fireballs but it won't hurt anyone but I can still use my telepathy. I'm sure everyone knows that we rejected Par Bliss or otherwise known as Warrior Heaven. When Neci stole our lives and we went to Par Bliss because we had done so many good deeds with our powers, we were offered a choice, to stay up there or on Earth. We chose to stay on Earth to keep doing good. We both chose the place where we were happiest and also so we can keep spreading our knowledge to new students like yourselves.

"Please don't worry if right now you don't like your powers, you feel a bit weird, you may not have wanted these powers. I had the most work to do in accepting myself because I hated my powers. But you will all come to a point when you will love your gifts and use them to do good and who knows, there may be a new group of Five Warriors here in this room," Niles glanced at Emily. "Now, what we need is for everyone to stand up in a straight line across the room."

The students got up and faced the Masonka wall that Cecil and Niles had appeared from. They were talking excitedly, honoured that they were being taught by legends. Cecil and Niles glided to the front of the room.

"Fireballs are an important part of battling and it's all about focusing your energy into a ball," Cecil said.

He held his hand out flat and a silver fireball the same size as a tennis ball, appeared in the palm of it.

"This is what we call a Baby Ball. It's nowhere near powerful enough to hurt anyone but it may leave a scratch. I want you all to produce one.

I AM . . .

The way to start is to think of something that makes you angry and focus all of that anger and want it to appear in your hand. It should, in the form of a Baby Ball."

The rest of the class was spent producing Baby Balls. Ambria Appleton from Berbinin was applauded for producing a Baby Ball on her first attempt but it was harder than Emily thought. She tried to focus all of her energy and recall as many bad memories as possible but she couldn't produce a Baby Ball.

Cecil, Niles and Master Zen were walking around the room, observing everyone's progress, although Niles's eyes had been on Emily since the task began.

"How's it going?" Niles asked Emily.

Emily grunted and flopped to the floor, "I don't know what's wrong. I can't do it."

Niles smiled at her, revealing adorable dimples in his handsome face, "There's no such thing as can't. Come on."

He watched her get back up and then stood next to her.

"I want you to focus with all your heart. You can do this!"

Emily focused and thought of as many memories that hurt her. Her palms were touching and were formed into a 'V' shape. Her arms were stretched out in front of her and she was crouched over. She stared intensely at the Masonka wall but still nothing happened.

Emily saw the surprised, almost worried look on Niles face, though he tried hard not to show it.

"That's very interesting," Niles frowned. "I'll be back to check on you later."

Emily slumped against the Masonka wall, staring at her hands, wishing that she could control her powers like the rest of the class could. Baby Balls were being shot all over the room and Emily watched enviously at everyone's progress. Emily stayed with her back to the wall until the lesson ended. Niles didn't come back to check on her.

As she walked in silence behind Michella, Wesley and Jason who were still buzzing from the lesson, Emily couldn't help but wonder. Seeing as she was Thomas's daughter, why didn't she have some form of advantage in terms of her progress as a warrior? Instead she feared that she would always be one step behind everyone else.

CHAPTER FIVE

Gossip

"Girl, you need to lighten up," Cathy snapped at Emily.

Emily sighed out of frustration and tried again to form a Baby Ball. They were both seated at the dining room table. Cathy was eating her cereal and was watching a half asleep Emily. She had been up half the night, practising her Baby Balls until she fell asleep and she still hadn't got it.

"Damn it," Emily shouted, when she failed again.

"Em, it was the first lesson, like come on, who else really got it?"

"Everyone," Emily replied.

"Oh. Well have some tea. You look like crap," Cathy said, pouring her a cup.

Emily shook her head, "I'll have some at school."

Sally beeped the car and Emily grabbed her school bag.

"I'm sure it'll be fine," Cathy said and Emily looked back at her with her eyebrows raised.

Rumours had spread through out the school that Emily couldn't produce a Baby Ball. She would walk down the halls to students laughing and effortlessly producing Baby Balls in front of her. Emily was so thankful for her friendship with Michella, Wesley and Jason who constantly stood up for her and calmed her down. More than once, Emily was tempted to knock everyone out.

The first flying lesson was with two other classes, Jenkint and Linktie, and Emily was dreading it. Flying sounded exciting and Emily had been thinking about it since she saw the cover of the school's prospectus, but after the Baby Ball incident, Emily felt insecure about her abilities and she hated the idea of embarrassing herself again.

At the breakfast table, all of the first years were talking about it non-stop, everyone except Emily.

"Cheer up," Jason said, with his mouth full of toast. "I don't know why you're so moody seeing as flying is the coolest thing to do."

"Jason," Michella hissed over the Daily Steward paper. "Leave her alone."

She turned a page in the paper and gasped, "Hey, look you're in the paper!"

Michella threw the paper in front of Emily. Emily feared for a split second it would be about the Baby Ball but when she glanced at the headline, it read. 'KNIGHT AT OSAKI,' followed by a picture of Emily with Jenny behind her, carrying bags from Warside.

"I didn't even see any cameras!" Emily said. "They're a bit late with the info. Clearly non-scandalous news can wait."

"Listen to this," Michella said. "The prestigious Osaki Training School has trained the world famous Five Warriors - Thomas Knight, Cecil Archinia, Niles Thompson, Hubert Jenkins and Roberta Taniana. The question to be asked is will Emily Knight, the daughter of Leah Knight and legendary hero and leader of the Five Warriors, Thomas Knight, be our new hero?"

Emily read the article over Michella's shoulder and snorted, "New hero? Are they taking the piss?"

The bell rang. Students were leaving for class but Emily, Michella, Jason and Wesley had a study period. Tanya Frank and her army of girls walked purposely past Emily.

I AM...

"Emily, are you excited about flying?" Tanya asked, smiling at her.

Emily noticed Tanya's friends, sniggering and nudging each other.

"Emily's the best flyer," Wesley said.

Emily caught his eye and he winked at her. "She flew all over the stadium last night."

Tanya's friends instantly stopped sniggering.

Tanya scowled at him, "Oh really, I thought you couldn't fly?"

She stared accusingly at Emily.

"Like I said, she's the best," Wesley said, putting his arm around Emily's waist. "So why don't you run along and you'll see later, won't you?"

Tanya looked from Wesley to Emily before turning on her heel and walking out of the dining hall with her friends behind her.

Emily hit Wesley on the arm as he released her.

"Ow, what was that for?" He rubbed his arm and took a step away from Emily.

"I can't fly you idiot! What did you go and say that for?" Emily shouted.

"Yeah Wes, I mean saying she's the best. It was a bit much," Jason said, flicking his fringe out of his blue eyes.

"Hey, what's all the negativity about?" Wesley said easily. "Come on, it's just flying. How hard can it be?"

At two o' clock, Emily and the rest of the Ogragon team headed towards the stadium, a five minute walk from the school. The sky was clear with a bit of wind, a perfect day to learn to fly.

Jenkint and Linktie were already on the sandy pitch in their white training kits. Ms Macay, the red-haired flying teacher arrived. Her square glasses were perched on the edge of her nose and her white training kit hung over her small frame.

"Hello class," she said happily. "I'm Ms Macay, team leader of Ogragon and the referee for the Dojo matches as well as your flying teacher. Flying is very simple. Does anyone already know how to do it?"

"Oh, great," Michella mumbled when she saw that most of the students had put their hand up.

"Good, well let's begin. Contrary to Foughtgon class, where you allow negative thoughts to boost your fighting power. To fly, you have to kick off from the ground, think positively and trust yourself. Let's take it in turns to go. Who would like to try first?"

A tall girl from Linktie announced that she was afraid of heights so Harmony Loving-Dale from Jenkint went first. She didn't seem to trust herself very much because she did a high jump and came back down. The class laughed and Ms Macay smiled at her.

"Maybe it would help if we all did it together," she told them, mainly to Harmony who shrugged it off. "On the count of three - one, two, three!"

"I can do this," Emily whispered to herself as she bent her knees and kicked off from the ground.

She couldn't believe she was flying. Emily expected to be scared but she wasn't, it felt as natural and easy as breathing. The wind was blowing in her face and she felt weightless. She could see the koi pond, the forest at the back of the school and the clear river that sparkled majestically in the sunlight. Emily was up much higher than everyone else. She looked down and could faintly see some students still on the floor. Emily felt someone barge into her back.

"What's your problem?" Emily yelled at Tanya Frank, who smirked at her.

"Well I definitely wouldn't say you were the best flyer here. Wesley clearly overrated you," Tanya drawled. "Interesting article this morning, don't you think? What did they say you were? The new hero?"

Tanya laughed loudly. "Some hero, can't even produce a Baby Ball, I heard."

I AM...

"Whatever," Emily said. She turned around and flew away from Tanya.

"I honestly feel sorry for you, Emily," Tanya said following her. "I was telling the girls this. I mean look, you have a Dad who would rather fly all over the world than look after you, a brother who ran away because he couldn't take the sight of you, and a Mum who's dead! Suicide seems likely -"

Emily spun around and flew at Tanya with her head down and head butted her in the stomach. Tanya crouched over, clutching her throbbing stomach and Emily punched her hard on her left cheek. Tanya screamed and began to fall but Emily held her up by her hair.

"Don't you ever, ever talk about my family like that!" Emily shouted in her face.

Emily released her and as Tanya started to fall, Emily flew after her. She wrapped her arm around Tanya's waist and with all of her energy, she dived as fast as she could to the ground, thumping Tanya's limp body into the sand. Powerful hands wrapped around Emily's waist and pulled her off Tanya, who was coughing up blood.

"Let go off me!" Emily roared. "I'm gonna kill her!"

"Stop, Emily!" Jason screamed, as he held on to her tighter.

"Fight, fight, fight!" students began to chant as they ran over, eager to see what was going on.

"Notting, let go of her," Ms Macay said, who stared at Emily with bulging eyes. "Knight! What do you think you're doing?"

Emily stood still breathing heavily. Her hair was matted to her forehead.

"She insulted my family."

"Go to room 102. NOW!" Ms Macay yelled.

Emily gave Tanya one last look as she withered on the floor before she turned on her heel and stormed up to the school.

Students watched curiously as an angry Emily marched up the stairs with sand covering her training kit. She walked through the empty corridors of the first floor and stopped outside room 102, where the name 'Ruth Walker' was inscribed. Emily started to panic when the realisation of what she had done hit her. What happened to students who made others cough up blood? Exclusion seemed to be the only option. Emily considered running to Michella's room but reconsidered it when she thought of how much trouble she would be in if she didn't see this Ruth woman. Emily knocked on the door.

"Come in."

She opened it to hear soft, gospel music playing. She looked around the carpeted room, filled from top to bottom with bookshelves, and saw two armchairs placed opposite each other in the centre of the room. In one armchair, was a middle-aged black woman. She wore small glasses and her dark hair was neatly brushed into a bun. She was a big woman. She was wearing a pretty pearl necklace over an orange cardigan. She was barefoot, her heels were dumped by the side of her chair. She had a folder on her lap and a pen in her hand. She looked up at Emily.

"Hello, Emily. Please sit down."

Emily didn't move, "How did you know my name?"

She pointed at the folder in her lap.

"I saw you all down there. That was some fight."

The woman pointed at her window and Emily groaned when she realised that it faced the pitch.

"And Ms Macay and I are also telepathic, so that helped too. Please, sit," the woman said, pointing at the chair opposite her.

Emily sighed and walked towards the seat. She could feel the woman studying her.

"My name is Ruth Walker and I am the school's counsellor -"

"Counsellor?" Emily interrupted.

Ruth peered at her over her glasses, "Yes, that's right. I'll be helping you like your counsellor at your godparent's. Jenny Li was her name, right?"

I AM . . .

Emily stared at Ruth, "How do you know that?"

Ruth picked up the folder in her lap and waved it, "We have a background check on every student."

"Is that code for using your telepathy to get into people's heads without their permission?" Emily spat.

Ruth smiled, "I don't abuse my powers Emily. Is there anything you want to talk about?"

"No," Emily said, picking the sand out of her fingernails.

"Emily," Ruth whispered and Emily looked up. "You just knocked out another pupil."

"She insulted my family," Emily said in a hard voice. "I didn't like it."

Ruth crossed her arms, "Do you want to tell me what happened?"

"No," Emily said getting up. "I don't even know you and you just expect me to tell you my business."

Ruth nodded and placed the folder on the floor, "You're right, Emily. You don't know me and I don't know you, but please understand that I'm here to help."

Ruth smiled at her and wrote something down in Emily's folder. The silence lasted for several minutes.

"Is that it?" Emily asked. She was starting to feel uncomfortable.

"Yes," Ruth said. "You're free to go. Why? Was there something else?"

Emily couldn't help but laugh, "I thought I was excluded or something."

"Would that have bothered you?" Ruth asked, looking at her with interest.

"I guess," Emily said shrugging her shoulders. "I mean, apart from Tanya, it's alright here. I also thought you were going to shout at me for injuring her."

"Do you want me to shout at you?" Ruth asked.

"No but I just thought you would."

"Did you enjoy hurting her?"

Emily shook her head, "No. I am sorry for hurting Tanya. Sometimes when I get really mad, it's like I can't control myself, like I'm a different person attacking."

Ruth wrote again in Emily's folder, "Have you ever played Dojo, Emily?"

"No," Emily replied. "Why?"

"You're free to go, Emily," Ruth said ignoring her. "Have a good day and I hope we can talk soon. My office is always open for you."

Emily nodded and hurried out of the door. The bell went off, signalling that the lesson was over. Emily sighed, almost certain that she would have to endure a couple of days of new gossip.

"There she is! Emily!"

Emily turned around and saw her foster brother, James waving at her. He was standing in between Cathy and Sally, who was wrapped up in an unflattering khaki jacket.

"Come meet my family quickly," Emily said to Michella, Wesley and Jason who were about to get on the coach to go back to St Bertudes Bus Station, so they could visit their families for the weekend.

Emily noticed as they got closer that Cathy was shortening her skirt and flicking out her curls.

"Nice legs," Wesley muttered to Jason.

"I heard that," Emily replied and the boys laughed.

"Hey James, Cath, Sally," Emily said, hugging them tight.

"Hello hun," Sally said, kissing the top of her forehead.

"These are my friends, Wesley, Jason and Michella. Guys this is my godmother, Sally and my sister, Cathy and my brother, James."

I AM . . .

They all said polite hellos to each other. Emily noticed Cathy looking back and forth at Wesley and Jason. A flirtatious smile playing on her lips. The boys kept glancing down at her toned legs.

"It's a bit cold to have the legs out, Cath," Emily teased.

Cathy shot her a dark look.

"Are you Emily's boyfriends?" James asked Jason and Wesley, who laughed.

"Yeah, mate," Wesley said and Emily nudged him.

"Ignore him, James. We're all friends," Emily said.

"It was really nice meeting you," Michella said smiling at Sally. "But our bus is going to leave. Emily we'll see you on Monday."

"Yep, see you guys," Emily waved.

Michella practically dragged the boys by their hands away from Cathy and Wesley looked back and winked at her. Cathy squealed loudly.

"Did you see that? Did you?" Cathy said, holding on to Emily's arm as they watched Michella, Wesley and Jason get on to the bus.

"Guys come on," Sally said, opening the car door.

"Which one do you like?" Cathy asked, when the car door was shut. "You sneaky girl. You didn't mention you were seeing hotties every day! Come on, I know you like one of them. What are they like?"

"Cathy give it a rest," Sally said, wearily from the front seat. "You should be asking her how school is and what she's been learning."

"In a minute, Mum!" Cathy snapped. "Your acting like *this* isn't important." She rolled her eyes before she grinned at Emily, "Tell me, tell me."

"We're just friends, Cath, all of us are."

"But what's the gorgeous blonde one like?" Cathy leaned in closer to Emily. "He looks like a model."

Emily nodded in agreement, "Yeah he's lovely but there's a very smart brain in there too so he'll see right through the little devious plans you have."

Cathy pouted, "Okay so the mixed race one? Those hazel eyes are amazing and his lips! Oh my gosh, don't you just want to grab him and kiss him?"

Emily laughed, "No! They're sweet but they're not really my type."

Cathy stared silently at her, "Mum stop the car."

"Why?" Emily, James and Sally asked.

"Because Emily likes someone," Cathy said, hitting her playfully. "Who is it? Damn I wish I went there, all those options."

"I do like someone," Emily began and Cathy clapped her hands. "I found out his name's Julian Kena but I've never even had a conversation with him so it's not a big deal."

"Well when you do, I want to be the first to know. Do you promise?" Cathy held out her little finger.

Emily looked at it and smiled, "I promise."

She linked her little finger with Cathy's.

Emily spent quality time with her family during her weekend, as she had no time on weekdays with the amount of homework she got. So she gossiped with Cathy about how gorgeous Julian Kena was and played 'Smash the Bricks' in the garden with the kids. She even flew around the garden for their entertainment. She told Jenny Li and Roberta Taniana about the school and the amazing lessons she had learnt. The only thing she left out was the Tanya episode and having to see a new counsellor.

The first lesson back at school was Meditation with Miss Amity Roshi. She was a petite lady with cropped dark hair and large brown eyes. She reminded Emily of a pixie. She was sitting cross legged with her back to the koi pond.

"Hello Ogragons, please remove your shoes and grab a zafu from the corner," Miss Amity Roshi said.

I AM...

"What's a zafu?" Emily hissed at Michella.

"I think it's one of them," Michella said, pointing at a pile of cushions in the corner.

Emily followed Michella and grabbed a red pillow and found a spot on the floor.

"Make sure you're comfortable on your zafu and sit with your legs crossed, back straight and with your hands on your knees," Miss Amity Roshi said.

Emily straightened her back and looked out on to the bridge that stood over the koi pond. The pink flowers from the tree were falling into the pond.

"I'm Miss Amity Roshi but please call me Roshi. Welcome to your first lesson of Meditation. In this class you'll learn subtle techniques that will help you as a warrior. Techniques such as breathing, clearing the mind of all thoughts, stretching and becoming more flexible," Roshi looked around the room. "This is all about relaxing your mind and your body, that's why this room faces the beautiful koi pond. After training so intensely on your physical strength, it's very important as warriors we give ourselves a chance to unwind so just copy my lead. Deep breath, in through the nose and out through the mouth . . ."

"Okay that was officially my favourite lesson," Jason said, as they walked to Flying.

"Only because we didn't do anything," Michella teased, nudging him. "It definitely is a nice change having to focus on relaxing and my body hasn't felt this loose in ages . . ."

Emily didn't see Tanya until a week later. She was strutting around the school, sporting a purple bruise on her cheek. When they passed each other in the hallway, Tanya gave Emily the dirtiest look she could master, echoed by her two friends but neither Tanya or her friends uttered a word to Emily.

During History class, the students were talking and reading magazines except Michella, Jason, stocky Adrian Mitchell and freckled Douglas Thornberry who were reading through a History book together. Mr King was playing chess with Danny June and Violet Hijen, Sarah John and lanky Melvin Cannon were playing hangman on the black board. A tall black boy knocked on the door.

"Sorry, Mr King, I need to borrow Emily Knight."

Emily looked up from her game of cards she was playing with Wesley and blonde haired Trevor Limted to see Michella's eldest brother, Lenny Kinkle, standing at the door.

"Yes, yes," Mr King murmured from under his black trilby hat, not even bothering to look up from the chess board.

Emily headed out of the classroom to a puzzled look from Michella. She stood opposite Lenny in the hallway.

"I got a letter from Ruth Walker a week ago and I've spoken about it with Ms Macay. Usually people have to audition but as captain I can fast track individuals if they're that good."

Emily frowned at him, "Sorry, what?"

"The Dojo team . . . didn't Ms Macay? Anyway, Ruth wrote to me last week about your fight with that girl." Emily hung her head. "And she said you fly well and you have a huge fighting power - not surprising - and you'd be good at Dojo and I think so too."

Emily looked at Lenny shocked, "Ruth nominated me to be on the team?"

"Well, yeah," Lenny said in a tone that suggested that anyone who made another student cough up blood during a lesson would be appointed. "Ms Macay was all for it. She and Ruth think that it would be a good way for you to release all that anger, and from what I hear you've got a lot of it. Plus, you have that Knight fighting power, are you in?"

Emily couldn't help but smile. She wasn't going to be expelled, she was going to play Dojo.

"Yes," Emily said. "I would really like that but I want to audition."

"What?" Lenny said, surprised.

"I want to earn my right to be on the team, not just because I'm Thomas's daughter."

Lenny scratched his head, "I've never heard of anyone not willing to be fast tracked. How about this, you come down to a training session and if you're good I'll keep you and if not, I'll search elsewhere?"

Emily nodded, "That sounds good."

Lenny smiled. "I hope you're as good as I think you are because our top fighter graduated last year and we've auditioned some really rubbish people. Err . . ." Lenny looked uncomfortable. "Were those rumours of the Baby Ball true?"

Emily's heart sank.

"Yeah, I'm kinda struggling with that."

"Oh, it's cool," Lenny said shrugging it off. "But you know what might help? Practising in the stadium in the evenings, when no one's around. Maybe not having any pressure will loosen you up, and training starts Friday."

Emily nodded. It wasn't a bad idea. Training with the team would start in a week and Emily was determined to get in by her own abilities.

"Hold on a minute, you made a girl go into hospital for a week and they reward you with a place on the Dojo team? That's not fair," Wesley complained.

"I'm not on it yet. I'm auditioning at the next training session," Emily said, as she devoured her corn on the cob.

"I think it's smart," Jason said.

Wesley glared at him. Jason put his hands up as if to surrender.

"No, hear me out. From a counsellor's point of view it makes sense. You have an angry student, you give them an angry sport to do, resulting in a less angry student."

"I wish I was good enough to play Dojo," Michella said, picking at her chicken. "Although playing with my brothers isn't my idea of fun."

Wesley sighed, "If I knew I could get picked to play Dojo by knocking someone out, I would have done it already. Damn you Emily, you always get there first."

Emily laughed as she tucked into her macaroni and cheese. Halfway through dinner, a bell rang. Emily checked her watch.

"Do we have another lesson?"

"No," Michella said "It's the post, look."

The four of them looked at the door and an army of students marched in with trolleys filled with letters and parcels. They stopped at almost every student, handing them an item.

Emily couldn't hide her surprise when a young Indian girl announced her name as she approached her with her trolley. Who would be writing to her at school? Emily raised her hand and the girl handed her a letter before strolling off. Emily ripped it open and a note the size of a business card was inside it.

"What does that say?" Wesley asked, as he picked at his chicken.

Emily pulled it out, "Meet me at Gilford's Walk in ten."

Emily turned it around but it wasn't signed. Michella looked at it over her shoulder.

"It's a bit messy for him but it could be Lenny, and look, he isn't even at the table."

Emily looked down the table and sure enough, Lenny wasn't there and neither were Warren and Pete, who she knew for a fact were on the Dojo team.

Emily finished her juice and stood up to leave, "Maybe it's a meeting or they're going to help me with my Baby Ball. Michael's picking me up late from work so I'm going to go and see what they want."

"Do you want us to come?" Michella asked.

"Yeah, why not."

Michella and Jason got up to leave with her. Wesley had to see Ms Macay about something he claimed to be top secret, so the three of them headed out of the school together. Gilford's Walk turned out to be the pathway that lead to the pitch. It was a cold evening and Emily still had on her training kit from Foughtgon class. Nobody was on Gilford's Walk.

"Should we walk up to the pitch?" Emily asked, looking around.

"No, let's wait here for a bit," Jason said, rubbing his arms.

They waited for fifteen minutes in the cold but there was no sign of Lenny or anyone else.

"He's taking the piss," Michella grumbled.

They turned to leave when Emily sensed a strong power behind her. She hurriedly pulled down Michella and Jason as a huge, blue fireball came shooting in their direction. It missed their heads by inches and flew into the darkness.

"What was that?" Jason asked, feeling his hair to check if it was singed.

"I don't know," Emily said, standing up. "Do you think that was Lenny? Maybe it's part of the audition?"

"It better not be. Lenny cut it out!" Michella hollered angrily.

"Who's that?" Jason asked. He pointed in front of them.

Emily looked up and saw a figure with long hair, standing and staring at them, not moving.

"D'you think it's Tanya?" Michella whispered.

"It can't be. She was at dinner and hey -"

The person suddenly turned and sprinted off in the opposite direction. Without thinking, Emily ran after the figure, to the dismay of Michella and Jason. They called out to her to stop as they ran after her.

A branch whipped Emily's bare cheek, making her wince in pain and she stumbled many times over stumps hidden in the dark. But still she followed the figure with the long hair. They were running deep into the forest at the back of the school. The faint calls of Michella and Jason fell on deaf ears as Emily didn't attempt to slow down. The person dodged effortlessly through trees and Emily struggled to keep her balance. She could barely see the person anymore.

Emily's throat was burning and a stitch in her torso forced her to stop and keel over, breathless. She couldn't hear any voices or footsteps. She glanced up and did a double take when she saw the person had stopped and faced her. The moon created unnatural shadows on the person's face so Emily could just see parts of it, like a jigsaw.

The figure began to walk towards her. Emily stood up and walked backwards, trying hard to stop shaking and control herself. She stumbled over a tree branch on the ground and fell hard on to her bottom and a branch cut across her calf. She cried out in pain and clutched her calf tight, rocking back and forth.

The person walked closer, out from the darkness and stepped into the light, so Emily could see him in his torn, muddy t-shirt and his bottoms, baggy and dirty. Her eyes widened in disbelief. She opened her mouth and no words came.

"Hi," he whispered in a small voice.

And Emily's eyes began to fill with tears, she couldn't believe what she was seeing. He was in front of her, staring at her. Her brother. Lox.

CHAPTER SIX

Revolution Night

"How did you get here?" Emily asked, looking up at him from the floor.

Her brother shuffled uncomfortably and shrugged his shoulders, "I teleported into the forest. I've been here since yesterday."

He walked towards her and Emily stared at him mesmerized. She couldn't believe he was standing in front of her after so long. Emily desperately wished she could somehow tell her Dad that Lox was here and that he could finally come home.

Lox held out his scratched and scarred hand and Emily grabbed it and together they managed to pull her up. A sharp pain shot through her calf and Emily buckled under her weight but Lox grabbed her before she fell. He pulled her close to him, hugging her tight. Emily wrapped her arms around his waist and squeezed him.

"You're so big now," Lox whispered into her hair. "I still think of you as my three year old sister who wouldn't stop crying - hey, don't cry Ems."

Emily wiped her wet face as she held Lox tighter, "I can't believe you're here. It's been so long."

"I know," Lox said softly.

They held each other in silence. Lox stroked Emily's hair affectionately. Emily breathed in his clothes. They smelt damp. Emily bit her lip as she wondered if she should ask the question she had been wanting to ask for years. Then she decided.

"Where have you been?" she asked.

"It doesn't matter," Lox said.

Emily pulled away and looked at him. His high cheekbones were still prominent under his caramel skin, making him look gaunt, and his scarred arms could be seen under his dirty t-shirt. His shoulder length, curly black hair was still knotty and his intense light brown eyes, that they had both inherited from their mother, looked back at her. There were also traces of their father which formed Lox's handsome face.

"What do you mean it doesn't matter? I haven't seen you for ten years. There's been at least one hundred million pounds donated for your safe return and here you are and you tell me it doesn't matter!"

"Keep your voice down. Someone will hear you," Lox hissed.

"Good!" Emily shouted. "I want the whole world to hear me. I want the world to see that you're back. I want them to know that my selfish brother left me and he's here and he can't even offer me an explanation!"

"It's complicated," Lox said, turning away from her.

"Really," Emily said, rolling her eyes. "How complicated is your life, Lox? Is it more complicated than mine? I have no mum or dad. I live with Sally and Michael and their foster kids. The whole world is watching me and knows every aspect of my life. HOW COMPLICATED IS YOUR LIFE, LOX?"

Lox stared at her silently before he turned and walked away from her. Emily threw up her hands and laughed, "Oh, I forgot. When Lox doesn't want to hear anything, there he goes. Well, piss off then!"

She watched as Lox stopped. He looked at her. His face was red. His eyes were large and hateful. He marched back to Emily, who took a step back. He stopped so they stood opposite each other.

"You don't know anything, Emily!" Lox screamed in her face. "You don't know a damn thing! I didn't have a lot of choices. So don't you dare tell me how complicated your life is! You don't know what life has been like for me."

"So, what has life been like for you Lox?" Emily asked calmly. "Because your hands are shaking."

Lox looked down at them, breathing hard. He clutched his hands into fists and squeezed them so they lost their colour. Emily and Lox looked at each other. They heard quick footsteps. They both looked towards the bushes near them.

"I know she came this way!" they heard Michella say.

"You can't tell them I'm here," Lox said, looking troubled.

"Why not?" Emily asked, in a hard voice. "It's your fault. You tried to knock us out with a fireball."

"I was trying to get your attention," Lox said. "Sorry it was stupid. How's your leg?"

"It's fine," Emily replied, in the same hard tone. "Why did you come, Lox?"

Lox sighed and brushed his hand hurriedly through his hair, "I came because I wanted . . . I mean, I need you to leave here and come with me."

Emily frowned, "Come with you where?"

"I can't say but I really need you to do that."

Emily laughed, "That information isn't very helpful. I mean, come on, Lox, are you serious? You won't even tell me why you left and now I'm meant to run away with you. Is this a joke?"

"Think about it Emily, we can be together. We can get to know each other again. We can even find Dad if you want and be a family again. I've seen all the headlines in the paper about you stealing and hurting people. It's all me and Dad's fault for leaving you like that, you should be with your family. You'd like that, right?" Lox said.

Emily bit her lip. He was offering her everything she wanted but there was something wrong. He looked too desperate, too pleading. She noticed his eyes kept darting around as if someone was there or was coming.

"Emily," Lox said, holding her hands. "I am begging you to please come with me. I don't want you to be hurt and the only way for you to be safe is to come with me."

"Safe from what?" Emily said, releasing her hands from him.

Lox glanced again at the bushes and then up at the inky sky. Emily walked towards him, her face softening.

"Lox, what's going on?"

Lox looked at her with wet eyes and a trembling body.

"She'll hear me," he whispered.

"Who?" Emily asked. "Please, Lox, let me help you."

She held out her hand towards him; he looked down at it. Emily didn't move. She prayed with all her might that he would take it. Lox slowly began to reach out his hand.

"Emily! Emily are you there?" Jason's voice rang loud and close.

Lox withdrew his hand. Emily ran up to him and gripped his arms tight.

"What's happened? What have you done? Why am I in danger? LOX TELL ME!"

Lox shook his head. He pushed Emily away from him and ran deeper into the forest. Emily fell on to the grassy floor. Another pain shot through her leg, making her cry out. She weakly called out to him but he didn't return.

"Emily!" Michella cried, as she and Jason emerged through the bushes with dirty clothes. They ran over to Emily who was crying loudly and Jason held her in his arms as she howled into his t-shirt.

Lox stopped when he heard her cry. He wanted to turn back, he wanted to go with her but he couldn't. She had made her choice and now Lox had made his.

It had been a week since Emily had seen Lox. Michella and Jason were still in the dark over what had made her so upset. Whenever they spoke of that night, Emily fell into a withdrawn state and would run off so they wouldn't see her tears. She wanted to tell them but Lox had asked her not to say anything and if he was in trouble, she didn't want to involve anyone else.

Emily had taken to walking on Gilford's Walk in the night, in an attempt to see him again. But he hadn't appeared. On one of her nights walking, she heard her name being called, but was disappointed to see it wasn't Lox but Lenny Kinkle.

"I've been looking for you everywhere," Lenny said, sounding breathless.

"Sorry," Emily said. "I didn't know."

"It's cool. Tomorrow night I need you to be at the stadium for six so I can go through the rules with you and audition you. Any luck with the Baby Ball?"

Emily shook her head, "No, sorry. I've been a bit off lately."

"Oh," Lenny said, looking worried. "Well, we're just going to have to practice it at training. Remember to wear your baht shoes."

Lenny waved at her and Emily continued with her walk. She had no sense of where she was going but her feet led her towards the stadium. Emily tugged at the door and it was open. She walked inside and looked around the stadium. A light was shining in the commentators' box and a figure was walking in it.

Emily's positive thought was when Sally gave her an old photograph of her Mum and with that happy feeling, Emily pressed down into the sandy floor and shot up into the sky, until she was above the stands. There were no other buildings near Osaki, just woodland and a huge mountain in the distance.

She stared at the mountain until she became restless. Then she began to circle the stadium until it became a big blur. Lox dominated her thoughts, which made her frustrated. *How could he leave me again?* She could see his face in her head and she clenched her fists tight. She screamed loudly but the anger and pain was still in her. She opened up her hands and saw two yellow Baby Balls seated in her palm. She looked at them and felt her anger leave her body as the Baby Balls grew bigger and bigger into fireballs. Emily turned her hands so the fireballs faced each other and she made them touch so they became one.

Emily's breathing became heavy as she watched her fireball, now triple the size of her head. She looked up to the sky and with all of her might, she threw the fireball away from her. It soared up high before it exploded and the stadium and Emily was covered in a blinding light.

The next evening before dinner, Emily made her way down to the stadium for her audition with the Ogragon Dojo team. When she got there, she saw a group of older students sitting on the sand. Warren Kinkle was laying on the ground and a beautiful, blonde girl, who was stretched out next to him, had her head resting on his stomach. Everyone else was sitting on the sand studying a large piece of paper.

Emily stood waiting awkwardly until Warren looked up and saw her.

"Hey, she's here. How's it going, Emily?"

"Good, thanks," Emily replied, aware of all the people staring at her.

She sat down next to Michella's other brother, Pete. Lenny stood up and looked around the group excitedly.

"Right, guys. Welcome back to the new term! This is Emily Knight for those of you who don't know her, although that's unlikely, and she will be auditioning today."

The team applauded and whistled loudly for her. Emily waved timidly.

I AM . . .

"Let me introduce the team to you. These lovely ladies are Summer Wind, Rosa Martin, and Raquel Davis."

Summer was the blonde girl lying on Warren's stomach, Rosa was a tiny, Italian girl with shoulder length, wavy, brown hair and small dark eyes and Raquel was black. She had a cropped hair style and piercings on her nose, ears and above her top lip. They all waved at Emily.

"They are Distracters and their job is to stick around throughout the match and distract your opponents, fight your opponents and other Distracters."

"And they're a little bit too good at distracting," Pete said before Raquel elbowed him.

"I'm hungry," a blonde haired boy with crutches said.

"Guys, focus," Lenny said, in a tired voice. "Okay, where was I? Oh yeah, Fighters can't hit the Distracters, only other Fighters and the aim of the game, as you most probably know, is to have the last Fighter standing in our team. You're instantly out once your feet touch the floor, regardless of whether you've been knocked out.

"Summer is our main Distracter, and of course you know I'm the captain," Lenny said smiling. "I was appointed this year so it's good we have a strong team. Usually females are Distracters but you'll possibly be our only girl Fighter and the fifth Fighter, so you end the battle. Everything depends on you."

"Don't scare her, Lenny," Rosa said.

"What exactly do I do? I've never played before," Emily asked as she tried to hide the panic in her voice.

"Well, you fight," Lenny said simply. "There are five rounds and myself, my brothers, Pete and Warren, Jessie Kendaschi and yourself fight a round each except Jessie's injured his knee so he's out this year."

Jessie lifted up one crutch and used it to wave at Emily, making her laugh.

"If your opponent knocks you out then the Fighter after you will have to finish your battle but in your case, Emily if you get knocked out the game's over and we lose."

The team looked at her and Emily became aware of the frightened look on her face.

"Err," Emily began, looking nervously at the floor. "You see, I've never battled before, so what exactly am I allowed to do?"

"Punch, kick, spit, bite, smack, rip, scratch -"

"Warren, enough," Lenny said holding out his hand to silence him. "We'll train you on how to battle properly and no one dies or anything, you might break a leg -"

"Or a tooth," Pete piped in.

"But," Lenny shot the pair a warning look. "It's all in good fun. You have a huge energy power so you're definitely capable and there's Reviving Water and the sick bay if you need it. But I'm sure you'll be fine," he added.

Emily nodded, even though she couldn't see the fun side of it.

"Okay, Emily. You're up against Warren and you need to get three hits in before he does but you have two minutes to do so. Let's go," Lenny said excitedly. When he caught sight of Emily's shocked face, he shrugged, "You wanted to audition."

The Ogragon Dojo team flew up high and made a wide circle around Emily and Warren who floated in the middle. Warren winked at Emily and Emily smiled nervously.

"Okay, go!" Lenny shouted.

Warren charged at her and Emily ducked and elbowed his back.

"Emily, one," Lenny said.

Warren shot a fireball at Emily that hit her in the arm. She clutched her arm and cried out.

"Warren, one. Shake it off Emily."

Warren moved so fast that Emily found it hard to track where he was. One second, he would be to her left, the next second on her right. Emily closed her eyes and could sense his power energy from behind. She swung her arms wildly and managed to hit Warren's chest as he teleported in front of her.

"Nice one!" Lenny shouted. "Emily, two."

The rest of the team were cheering them both on. Emily was breathing heavily. Just one more hit and she was in. Warren threw a punch at her and Emily blocked it. He spun around and kicked Emily's head. The impact made her fly back but she was caught by Rosa.

"Wow, that hurt," Emily said, shaking her head.

"Watch out!" Rosa said.

A yellow fireball flew towards them. Emily flew away from it but when she turned around, the fireball was still behind her. She dived and it went with her. Emily gritted her teeth and flew faster around the stadium, she could feel the heat of the fireball on her back. She spotted Warren laughing as he controlled his fireball and an idea came to her. Emily did another lap around the stadium. Warren was laughing so hard, he wasn't focusing on where Emily was flying. She took her chance and dived towards Warren and before he noticed, she grabbed him in a hug and spun him around, so the fireball hit him in the back. Warren yelled and Emily let him go, so he fell towards the floor and landed on the sand.

The rest of the Ogragons applauded Emily and Lenny reached out his hand towards her, which Emily shook.

"Welcome to the team."

Once Warren had had his Reviving Water and was fully healed, they spent the rest of the lesson sparring against one another with Lenny shouting corrections in Emily's ear. It took a while for Emily to learn to ignore Summer, Rosa and Raquel flying around and shooting random fireballs at her, but once she got used to it, she learnt to use them to her advantage. Emily had trouble producing her Baby Ball on demand but she promised a horror stricken Lenny that she could do it. She just needed more time and practice. So she hoped.

By the end of the month, thoughts of Lox weren't as frequent. Lessons were getting harder and Dojo practice was every other day, so Emily was either busy doing homework or training. The training was taking a toll on her body. Emily was in constant pain, which was affecting her sleep and she sometimes fell asleep in lessons. Most of the teachers were very understanding, apart from Mr Waternham who taught Water Studies.

Emily hated the sound of the subject from the start. Mr Waternham told the class that every warrior has the natural ability to breathe under water. They would spend the year learning to breathe and building their confidence under water, as it was easier said then done and those who progressed would learn to battle under water.

Emily had hated water since the age of nine, when she almost drowned in her indoor swimming pool so the idea of being under water filled her with dread. Emily couldn't grasp how it was possible for warriors to breathe under water and truthfully she didn't want to try it out to see if she could.

It had been months since Emily had started Water Studies and she had still not mastered breathing under water. She was sitting in the corner watching Michella climb into the see-through tank. Emily yawned. She was finding it hard to focus. She rested her head against the wall and closed her eyes.

"Miss Knight!"

Emily jumped up.

"I hope you were looking closely at Miss Kinkle. It's your turn."

"Crap," Emily muttered.

She walked slowly to the tank avoiding her classmates' eyes. She bent her legs and flew up, hovering over the tank as Michella had done. Emily looked down at the water and groaned. She slowly lowered herself so she was in the warm water. Emily took quick, deep breaths and looked pleadingly at Mr Waternham.

"All the way in," he said, with his arms crossed.

Emily sighed and took a deep breath and went under. The water instantly ran up her nose and into her ears. She opened her mouth a little bit and the water gushed in. Emily swam to the surface and coughed violently and spat out the water.

"Mr Notting, can you educate Miss Knight on why she can never drown?" Mr Waternham said to Jason, who caught Emily's eye and blushed.

"Because when water enters our mouth, we have a gag reflex. Parts of our throats close, so water can't enter. It's the same reason why babies can breathe under water?"

"Did you hear that Miss Knight? The same thing a *baby* can do, so next time pay attention or I'll make sure you're left under the water," Mr Waternham said.

Jason caught her eye again and mouthed, "Sorry."

At dinner, Laton Chin mentioned a costume party on Revolution Night. It was a night to celebrate the leaders of the Warrior Revolution, Idris Jenkint, Bernard Ogragon, Rose-Marie Mentorawth, Joseph Berbinin, Arthur Linktie and Ce-Ce Pentwon and would be held in a few weeks. It was a tradition at the school but most of the first years were oblivious to this. So for the next two weeks, first years were found in the hallway with fabric and scissors attempting to make something original in between lessons.

Pete Kinkle kindly gave Emily and Michella some material to make costumes out of, but when questioned on how he managed to purchase the fabric, he made a hurried excuse and left them.

On the last Friday of the month, after their last lesson, students were running into their team rooms so they could have plenty of time to get ready. The girls' room was mayhem. There were different coloured materials covering the floor and all types of make-up and face paint covering the beds.

Emily was facing the mirror in Michella's bedroom. She had managed to secure her long hair into the neatest bun she could master. She admired her torn yellow dress and sprinkled glitter all over herself.

"Your wings fell off," Michella said to Emily, as she helped secure her cardboard wings.

"Thanks, I like your hair," Emily said, admiring Michella's ringlets.

Michella tossed back her hair dramatically and Emily laughed.

"Do you think it's bad that we're all dressed as fairies?" Violet Hijen asked, as she put her hair into pigtails. "Isn't it a bit lazy?"

"Well it was your idea," Nicky Johansen said. "Besides, I think it's cool. Only the Ogragon first years are cool enough to be fairies and if we see any others trying it, we'll break their wings."

The girls laughed. A knock came at the door.

"Come in," Daisy Atam cried.

Two handsome boys in suits and sunglasses opened the door and the girls squealed excitedly.

"You're all fairies. That's original," Wesley said sarcastically.

"Leave off," Sydney John said, as she applied her mascara. "We look hot and you know it."

"Yes clearly I can't control myself," Wesley said, rolling his eyes.

"I didn't know you had a suit?" Michella asked.

"My Gran had it hidden away," Wesley said.

"Does your Gran live with you?" Emily asked intrigued.

Wesley nodded, "Yeah since my Mum went to rehab."

"What do you think of my costume Jason?" Sarah John asked, showing off her dress which revealed a toned, flat stomach.

Jason smiled, "It's cute."

"Really?" Sarah smiled. "Maybe we should go down together then?" She fluttered her fake eyelashes at him.

"Err," Jason said, backing away. "No can do babe. I'm Jewish and my Mum only likes me dating Jewish girls. Religion and all that. Let's go Wes."

Jason pulled on Wesley's sleeve and hurried Wesley out of the door. Wesley was covering his mouth, trying to hold in his laughter. A bemused Sarah turned to Michella.

"I didn't know Jason was a Jew."

"Yeah he is," Michella replied and when Sarah went back to doing her hair, she whispered to Emily. "When it suits him. He only throws that out when he has no interest in the girl."

"So why didn't he just say no?" Emily frowned.

Michella raised her eyebrows, "That's one thing Jason finds hard to say and as for his Mum being pissed off, we used to date and I'm as Jewish as a Buddhist!"

"You dated Jason?" Emily squealed. "You didn't say."

Michella smiled slyly, "That's another story babe."

The party was in the Foughtgon room and it looked amazing. The cream walls and the Masonka wall were covered with white curtains and there was a giant disco ball hanging from the ceiling making the lights skim across the curtains. The Reviving Water buckets and blue mats were cleared out of the way, leaving space for dancing and there were plates of food and drinks on one table at the end of the hall.

Emily was amazed by the costumes. There were vampires, Five Warrior lookalikes, secret agents but she was ecstatic to see that only the first year Ogragon girls were fairies. They joined the crowded hall and began to dance to the loud music. Emily walked sideways (to avoid anyone knocking off her wings) towards the table with the food. She was eyeing up the large chocolate cake in the centre when someone tapped her shoulder.

Two people were standing in front of her with black robes on, carrying a head in their left hands. There wasn't a head on the top of their cloaks. Emily screamed loudly but was barely heard over the music.

"Why are you screaming?"

Two heads popped out of the clocks and grinned wickedly at her. Emily punched Warren and Pete on the arm and they laughed.

"Idiots! You bloody scared me!" Emily yelled at them.

"But you can't deny these are great," Pete said.

Emily couldn't help but smile as she studied their life like sculptures which resembled both of them amazingly. The boys walked off towards Michella, hiding their heads again. Emily turned back to the cake. She cut herself a huge piece.

"Hi, Emily."

Emily looked to her right to see a boy with a black masquerade mask on, that covered his eyes. His long black hair was plaited neatly into a ponytail. It was Julian Kena. She quickly halved her enormous piece and put it back.

"Hi, Julian," Emily smiled. "That's a great costume."

"Thanks, yours is cute."

Emily blushed, "Do you want some cake?"

She offered out some of hers.

Julian shook his head, "I'm good thanks."

They stood in silence. Wesley danced past them with a blonde haired girl from Jenkint called Harmony Loving-Dale. Emily glanced at Julian who was already staring back at her. Emily felt herself turn red. He smiled

I AM...

at her and touched her hand gently before he walked off. Emily took a deep breath in and fanned her hot face. She poured herself a glass of juice and went back on to the packed dance floor to try and find her fairy crew. In front of her was a tall person in a black hooded robe.

"Excuse me," Emily shouted but the music drowned her out.

Emily tapped the person's shoulder with her free hand. The figure in black turned to look at her.

"Hi, can I get through?"

The black mask on its face hid any form of friendliness.

"I've been waiting for you," the person hissed softly.

"What?" Emily shouted. "I can't hear you, the music's too loud!"

The person grabbed Emily tight around the neck and picked her up. The grip was so tight that Emily could hardly breath. Emily dropped her glass and cake. The glass hit the floor and broke but no one seemed to notice; they were too busy enjoying themselves.

Emily scratched at the hands around her neck but the grip only got tighter and Emily had to take in small gasps of air to breathe. Her neck was starting to hurt. She couldn't breathe properly. She didn't understand why no one was helping.

Anger seeped through Emily's body and she felt her hands heat up and she fired a fireball at the person's stomach. The figure let go of her immediately and flew towards the wall, knocking people out of the way and the figure banged its back and fell to a clump on the floor. Emily dropped on her hands and knees, taking in short, fast breaths. She gently felt her neck. It felt bruised and raw. The hall erupted with voices. Everyone wanted to see and know what was going on.

"Oh my gosh Emily, are you alright?" Michella asked anxiously, running over and putting a protective arm around her shoulders. "I didn't even see. What happened?"

Emily nodded, "I'm okay . . ."

She stopped and watched the person in black stand up. It stretched its arms out and fired two large, purple fireballs. Students ran out of the way, screaming and pushing one another. One fireball flew to the white curtains, which erupted in a golden flame and the other hit the table at the end of the hall which blew up. Food and drinks soared into the air and landed on the floor, on the walls and on the students.

"Fire!" someone yelled over the screams.

"Where's the headmaster?" a girl screamed. "Get Mr Davon!"

The person in black took strong, quick strides towards Emily. Students were running out of the hall. Teachers and students were firing fireballs at the person, who dodged and rebounded them effortlessly. The figure was inches away from Emily. Michella tried to pull her up but fear kept Emily still. She felt a strong hand touch her shoulder and she looked up to see the headmaster, Mr Davon standing in front of her in an emerald training kit. His blonde, grey hair was slicked back into a ponytail. He stood tall and fearless, his blue eyes stared down at the impostor. The person took a step back, swung its black cloak and teleported.

"Students," Mr Davon barked over the noise as Ms Macay ran into the hall and poured water over the smouldering curtains. "Stay in this hall. Cecil, Niles and teachers check around the school and grounds and make sure whoever it was has gone and any students you see, report them to the hall at once."

"Yes, sir," the teachers chorused before they teleported.

"Students, do not be frightened, everything is okay," Mr Davon said.

He walked over to the DJ and whispered something in his ear and the music blared back on.

"There's no reason why your party shouldn't continue," he shouted over the music before he teleported also.

Everyone stared at Emily. All she could hear were whispers around her, some people were even pointing. Tears were running down her face.

I AM...

"Let's get out of here," Jason said, who was standing by her side.

"Mr Davon said to stay in here," Michella protested.

"She can't stay in here with everyone staring, can she?"

Wesley helped her up and held her tight. She didn't realise she was shaking as Jason led them out of the room. For them, the party was over.

CHAPTER SEVEN

Dojo

It was the middle of November and the hot topic amongst the students was still Emily and the Revolution Night intruder. Emily found herself shunning the Ogragon living room and the dining room when it was too busy, to get away from the curious stares and awkward questions. She stopped hanging around after school and instead chose to go straight home. She was grateful the press hadn't got wind of it and she refused to worry Sally and Michael.

Emily found herself talking less to Jenny and visiting Ruth Walker regularly since the incident. Emily found it easier to open herself up to Ruth. Ruth understood her better than Jenny because she was also a warrior and while everyone else had unreachable expectations for Emily and judged her every move, Ruth had no judgement. Ruth always listened patiently and because she was a Christian, Ruth always gave her Biblical references. She told Emily that God had blessed her with a gift and God wouldn't have given it to her if she couldn't handle it. Emily found that hard to believe. If it was a gift, then why didn't she know *how* to handle it?

It was after a very intense afternoon of Dojo training and Emily was seated at dinner in between Wesley and Jason. The headmaster, Mr Davon, walked to the front of the hall in a fitted, scarlet red, training kit, that showed off his athletic body. His blue eyes sparkled as he waited till he had everyone's attention.

"The Dojo trials are over, so if you didn't make the team please do try again next year. I would like everyone to help me celebrate those who did make the team."

Mr Davon pulled out a piece of paper from his pocket.

"For the Jenkint team, second year, Kent Brod -"

A short mix raced boy, with blonde, curly hair stood up.

"And first year, Jeff Wilson."

A white boy with freckles stood up followed by a round of applause from the students. Emily noticed Harmony Loving-Dale, whose long blonde hair was covered in beads. Emily remembered that Wesley had danced with her at the Revolution Night party. Harmony whistled loudly for the new Jenkint Dojo team members.

"For the Linktie team, forth year, Craig McNeon and first year, Tanya Frank."

Tanya waved her hand as if she was royalty.

"Tanya?" Wesley said, in disbelief. He cupped his mouth and booed loudly at her, making everyone laugh.

"For the Berbinin team, first year, Ambria Appleton and fifth year, Andy Carmichael."

Everyone applauded them.

"For the Pentwon team, second year, Lucy Carth.

Emily clapped whilst eyeing up the girls that were called. Secretly relieved that they weren't giant, Amazonian woman but they were skinny and small like her.

"For the Mentorawth team, we have two first years, Betty-Sue Thompson and Julian Kena and forth year, Sylvia Lee-Smith."

The Mentorawths cheered loudly. Julian blushed as he stood up. Emily clapped extra hard when she saw him and Wesley raised his eyebrows at her.

"And lastly, congratulations to Lenny Kinkle for being appointed captain and for their newest member, first year Emily Knight."

A roar of applause came from the Ogragons who drummed on the table and stamped their feet on the floor. Michella pushed Emily up and Lenny stood up at the opposite table and the applause got louder. Tanya looked shocked when she saw Emily whilst Julian stuck two thumbs up at her.

Mr Davon held up his hand and the hall fell silent, "This Friday, the first Dojo match of the season will commence with Ogragon against Mentorawth at noon. Good luck to both teams."

There was a last round of applause. Emily caught Julian's eye again and he smiled at her. Emily smiled back and prayed her powers wouldn't let her down in front of the entire school.

The evening before the match, Emily deserted the dinner table early as she planned to take a walk to the stadium to collect her thoughts. As she turned the corner, she saw Cecil and Niles hovering near the entrance doors, bent close to each other. Emily hesitated whether to interrupt and say hello but then Niles spoke with a raised voice.

"You can't ignore the fact she couldn't produce a Baby Ball Cecil! I know she's got a high energy level but maybe she's not as good as Thomas and Lox. Maybe we're expecting too much from her. Maybe Roberta's wrong."

Cecil shook his head with a solemn face, "Roberta hasn't been wrong yet. Let's not write her off just yet Niles. Tomorrow at the match we will see her progress."

Emily quietly retraced her steps back around the corner before breaking into a run. She passed the packed dining hall and went straight to Michella's room which was empty. Emily sat on Michella's bed and stared at the pitch through the window. She imagined it packed with people and everyone watching her fight. How many of them would compare her to Thomas and Lox?

There was a knock at the door and it opened slightly.

"Hello? Emily?"

Emily looked and saw Wesley at the doorway, squinting at her through the dimly lit room.

"I saw you run past the dining hall. You missed the apple crumble and ice cream. You okay?" he asked kindly, as he walked in.

She nodded her head as he sat down next to her on her bed.

"So what's all this?" he said, wiping away a tear that trickled down her cheek.

"I don't know," Emily said, shrugging her shoulders. "PMS or something."

"Really?" Wesley asked, slowly moving away from her and Emily couldn't help but laugh.

"Wesley, I don't think I can do this match tomorrow. What if I'm rubbish? And I get Ogragon kicked out from the first match?"

"You'll be great," Wesley protested. "Everyone's well excited about seeing you tomorrow."

"But if I lose," Emily said, looking at him with her eyes wide and wet. "Everyone's going to hate me. What if I'm not good enough? And I'm not as good as Lox and my Dad?"

Wesley stared at her sadly before he kissed her softly on the forehead. Emily looked at him surprised.

"Sorry, I do that to my little sister when she cries."

"It's okay," Emily said smiling. "I didn't know you had a sister."

"Didn't you? Her name's Cammie. She's best mates with Michella's sister, Madison. What with Mum not being around and our Dad, who left us years ago, I get used to dealing with upset girls."

Emily looked out of the window, "It must be tough dealing with your Mum's alcoholism. You never seem sad or angry. How do you do that?"

Wesley laughed, "Trust me when I was younger, I went a bit crazy. I even tried drinking myself just to see what the big fuss was about. I hated it. But when Mum saw how much I was spiralling out of control, she agreed to go to rehab. Then my Nan came and now everything's better."

"That's good," Emily said.

"Yeah but I do worry about Cam a lot. That's why I go home at weekends because I need to see her and make sure she's okay. She's only nine so she thinks I'll disappear like Mum and Dad did . . ."

Emily reached in the darkness and found Wesley's hand. She squeezed it tight and he squeezed back.

"You're a good brother. You're how a big brother's meant to be. She's lucky to have you."

"Thanks," Wesley said, smiling. "She's going to like me even more."

"Why?"

"I'm commentating the Dojo matches with Harmony. You know Harmony right? And they're paying me for it so that can help my Nan and Cammie out."

"Oh that's great Wes. Seriously, you're amazing."

Emily was surprised to feel her heart race as Wesley looked at her. His hazel eyes locked on to hers. They both turned away at the same time. Emily felt herself blush. She looked down and stared at their interlocked fingers.

Emily awoke with a sick feeling in her stomach when she thought of the match that would take place that afternoon but she put it aside and quickly got dressed. She snuck out of the house and ran to Roberta and Jenkins'

house. She had to find out what Roberta had seen in her vision to worry Cecil and Niles so much. She knocked on the door of their white mansion but no one answered. She banged on it and hollered, "Aunt Roberta! Uncle Jenkins!" but still no one answered. Emily sighed and ran back to her house.

"Where did you go?" Sally asked, when Emily walked through the front door.

"To see Aunt Roberta but she wasn't in."

"Oh they've gone on one of their publicity tours, they won't be back for a while."

"Great," Emily muttered. She grabbed her bag and followed Sally to the car.

Emily sat silently in the school dining hall with a plate full of food in front of her. Wesley had already eaten his food and left the hall with Harmony. Emily refused to eat. She felt sick with nerves. She wanted the match to be over and done with.

"Stop worrying Emily, you're going to be fine," Michella said, before she picked up the paper that was on the table.

"Easy for you to say, you're not the one that's going to get beaten up in front of the whole school," Emily replied bitterly.

"Positive attitude," Jason sang. He buttered her a piece of toast. "Eat."

She took a small bite when Ms Macay approached her.

"Knight, make your way to the stadium."

Emily nodded. She took another quick bite as her table wished her good luck and Emily knew that not even luck would save her now.

Twelve o'clock struck and the stands were filled with students and teachers. Michella and Jason were seated next to Sydney John and Danny June. They had grabbed seats in the middle of the stands, perfect for when the players flew up. Wesley was at the very top with Harmony Loving-

Dale from Jenkint. They were in a booth so they couldn't be disturbed and they stared intensely at the pitch.

Meanwhile, the Ogragon Dojo team had just finished putting on their black baht shoes and crimson Dojo uniform. The cheers and yells from the stadium could be heard from the changing room. Emily gulped down her water to calm her nauseated stomach. Lenny let out a deep sigh.

"Okay team, this is the first match of the new season and I don't know about you guys but I think we can win this year."

The team cheered. Emily's nerves got in the way of her enthusiasm.

"You all know the strategies and we've been training so hard. I know we're one man down but we're still blessed. Do your best and good luck."

Emily followed Warren out on to the pitch. Thunderous cheering echoed throughout the stadium. Everything was a blur to Emily. She kept her eyes forward and ignored her racing heart, instead she listened to the students chanting for Ogragon.

"And here's the Ogragon team," Wesley reported. "Lenny Kinkle, Summer Wind, Raquel Davis, Rosa Martin, Pete Kinkle, Warren Kinkle and Emily Knight."

The Ogragons cheered passionately and the Mentorawths walked on to the pitch in midnight blue followed by applause from the students.

"And here's the Mentorawth team," Harmony announced. "Vince King, Jansi Edge, Sylvia Lee-Smith, Betty-Sue Thompson, Tommy Anderson, Eddie Hunting and Julian Kena. Forth year, Ritchie Guns isn't playing today as Ogragon are one fighter down because of Jessi Kendashchi's broken leg."

The Mentorawths lined up opposite the Ogragons. Julian stared sternly at Emily, who looked away nervously. Ms Macay, the referee stood in between the teams.

"I want a clean match," Ms Macay ordered. "Stick to the rules and set an example for the rest of the season. Ferguson Cloud is on hand to give out Reviving Water."

I AM . . .

She pointed to a large, ginger man wearing a black puffa jacket.

"On the whistle fly up and I'll whistle when it's time for the next fighter to battle. Three-two-one."

The whistle blew shrilly and Emily kicked up from the ground. The wind blew uncomfortably in her face and through her training kit. Emily shivered as she hovered with her team away from the centre of the pitch where Lenny and the Mentorawth captain, Vince King sized each other up.

"And here we go," Wesley reported. "Ms Macay's blown the whistle and Vince King aims a punch at Lenny Kinkle - but oh he's missed and what a great kick to the chest from Kinkle. King is down - but no, he's back up, he's heading straight for Kinkle - he's punched him right in the head too, ooh that's going to be sore tomorrow. Summer Wind, Ogragon's lead Distracter has just shot a huge fireball at new first year, Betty-Sue Thompson, Distracter for Mentorawth - oh and Thompson's falling fast - she's hit the ground and she's out of the game. Go Ogragons!"

There was a roar of applause from the crowd followed by hisses from the Mentorawths. Emily watched as Ferguson waved a blue flag and gave Betty-Sue Reviving Water and seconds afterwards, she was conscious and watching the match. Harmony continued the commentary.

"Ogragon Distracters, forth years, Raquel Davis and Rosa Martin are charging towards King - but here comes Mentorwaths Distracters, Jansi Edge and their newest recruit, Sylvia Lee-Smith who are blocking them - a punch from Davis to Lee-Smith and Edge has kicked Martin in the stomach and they're all at it! Three battles at once and the crowd are loving this! Kinkle's gone after King and King's teleported - right in front of Wind! Big mistake! King's just realised, he's turned to Wind who's kicked him in the - oh dear! King's keeled over and Kinkle's taken advantage with a tremendous fireball and . . . is he falling? Yes, he is! KING IS OUT OF THE GAME! OGRAGON TAKES THE LEAD!"

There was another loud cheer from the crowd. Emily cheered also but she noticed Lenny was flying slower than before. The boos from the Mentorawths echoed throughout the stadium. Vince King hit the ground with a loud thump and Ferguson looked at him before holding up a red flag, making the Ogragons cheer louder.

"The flag's up - Kinkle won that round and there's the whistle - it's Eddie Hunting from Mentorwath - poor Kinkle looks tired but that's what happens in a game of Dojo. Hunting's got the upper hand - Lee-Smith has just flown by Kinkle, did she just touch up his leg? Kinkle's distracted, don't blame him, I'd be distracted too."

"Seeing as Wesley's drooling," Harmony laughed. "I'll commentate. Hunting is still controlling this match - an uppercut to Kinkle's chin and is that blood? Lee-Smith's back shooting dozens of Baby Balls at Kinkle so he's hidden behind the smoke - where are the Ogragon Distracters? Hunting's fired a red fireball into the smoke - Rosa Martin and Raquel Davis have barged Lee-Smith leaving Hunting with Kinkle - Hunting's spinning and double kicked Lenny straight in the face and he's falling - he's on the ground - the red flag's up. KINKLE IS OUT OF THE GAME! ONE ALL!"

There was a loud roar from the Mentorawths. Wesley swore loudly into his microphone which echoed throughout the stadium. Emily laughed; Harmony elbowed him. Ms Macay shot him a warning look before she blew her whistle and Pete Kinkle stepped out to continue the battle with Eddie Hunting.

"Look how fast the two of them are fighting - Hunting with the upper hand - not for much longer 'cause Wind's behind him and she elbowed him right on the back of his head - Hunting spun round, big mistake - Kinkle's taken advantage with a dig to the back and another elbow to the head - Hunting looks dizzy - Kinkle's circling Hunting - he's a blur and fireballs are shooting from his hands - Hunting's trying to fight against it but is failing miserably, Hunting's touched the floor - the flags up - HUNTING'S OUT OF THE GAME! 2-1 TO OGRAGON!"

The Ogragons stamped their feet on the stands and a deafening roar of applause echoed through the stadium. Emily saw Julian put his head in his hands. Emily couldn't help but smile as she heard Wesley sing, "Oh happy day," over the microphone.

The whistle blew again and Tommy Anderson from Mentorawth stepped out. The match didn't last very long. Pete beat Tommy easily but got knocked out by stocky Ritchie Guns. Warren was next to take on Ritchie.

In the middle of their battle, Warren fired a huge fireball at Ritchie. Ritchie crossed his arms over his face to rebound it but he still got knocked back because of its power. The fireball rebounded off Ritchie and flew back to Warren, who didn't move fast enough and the fireball hit him on his chest. They both fell and hit the floor at the same time which resulted in a Double K.O. Two red flags went up.

"So the match now lies on the shoulders of these two young debut fighters. Mentorawths, Julian Kena!" Harmony said.

Julian flew to the centre of the stadium to a round of applause. The Mentorawths were chanting his name.

"And Emily Knight!"

Even over all of the cheers, Emily could distinguish Michella and Jason's. She faced Julian. He smiled at her; Emily barely returned it.

Ms Macay blew the whistle and Julian swiftly charged at Emily. Emily screamed and flew out of the way quickly. Julian followed her. He caught her arm, spun her around and punched her hard in the stomach. Emily couldn't breathe. She was knocked back with so much power that she flew across the stadium and banged her back against something solid. Emily could feel eyes and voices surrounding her. Only when someone hit the invisible wall to get Emily's attention, she realised that the stands were covered to protect the audience from the fight. Wishing that she could be protected from Julian, she only just looked up in time to see Julian charging towards her, fists clenched and she flew out of the way.

"Lucky escape by Knight, Kena's bounced off the wall - trying to get a punch at Knight but she's cleverly dived under his legs - she's behind him - she's elbowed the back of his head and she's flown up and shot back down kicking Kena's back - is he? Yes, he's falling fast, he's nearly touched the floor - HE'S BACK UP!" Wesley said in disbelief.

"What?" An astonished Emily shouted over the crowds cheers.

Julian looked tired and in pain but he flew back to Emily and winked at her.

"Distracters Sylvia Lee-Smith and Janis Edge have taken advantage of the situation, they have all shot their fireballs at Summer Wind - she hasn't seen it and it's hit her right in the back too - Raquel Davis and Rosa Martin have just realised but it's too late - Wind's touched the ground - the blue flag's up. She's out of the game and Davis and Martin look livid!"

Emily glanced down at Summer sprawled on the floor, her blonde hair covering what Emily knew would be a raging face.

"Davis has shot a large fireball at Lee-Smith - she's caught it! LEE-SMITH HAS CAUGHT THE FIREBALL!" Harmony announced, sitting on the edge of her seat. "Martin's attempting a sneak attack on Lee-Smith - but Lee-Smith has caught her fireball as well. SHE'S CAUGHT TWO FIREBALLS! This is insane! And now's she combined the two to make a giant fireball. Wesley, what do you think they should do?"

"They should leg it," Wesley said. "They should just fly away in different directions then she won't know who to shoot the fireball at. Knight and Kena are still fighting and Kena is dodging all of Knight's punches - where is he getting this energy from? I would get him tested. Davis and Martin have put their hands together and made their own fireball - not as big as Lee-Smith's - come on girls, bigger! Edge has added her energy to Lee-Smiths and - oh crap, this doesn't look good."

I AM . . .

Lee-Smith's fireball had grown bigger than her body. Emily and Julian stopped fighting and looked at the red fireball, which was growing bigger by the second. Emily flew over to Raquel and Rosa and Emily held the fireball as Raquel and Rosa powered up and shot their fireballs into it, it was getting big but not big enough.

"More, come on!"

"We can't, Emily," Rosa said panting, her face was shiny with sweat. "That's all we've got."

"Ladies - look."

Raquel was pointing at the Mentorawths and Julian was adding his fireballs to Lee-Smith's one. Emily looked at the blue one in her hands and she concentrated hard.

Come on, just one fireball, she said to herself but it didn't matter how hard she prayed and pushed, not one fireball emerged from her hands. She looked up and gasped. The Mentorawths had released the fireball and the red inferno was charging towards them.

CHAPTER EIGHT

Revelation

Emily felt like everything was moving in slow motion. The Mentorawths' red fireball easily overshadowed Emily, Raquel and Rosa. Emily glanced at Raquel and Rosa's terrified faces and she knew there wasn't anything left they could do. Emily shot their blue fireball; it flew rapidly and hit the red fireball with a deafening boom. The fireball was starting to burn Emily's hands and the red fireball was overpowering theirs effortlessly. The red fireball's power was pushing Emily slowly down to the floor.

"Emily, move!" Raquel shouted.

"I can't," Emily groaned. "It's too powerful."

"If you touch the floor, we've lost. We'll take care of this, you take care of Kena," Rosa said. She looked worried but her voice was strong and steady.

Rosa and Raquel flew on either side of Emily. The force of the fireballs had created an unnatural wind, making the sand from the floor rise up and swirl around them, blinding them. Emily couldn't see anything but the sand and the fireball. Raquel and Rosa were nowhere to be seen. Rosa flew towards Emily and she pushed her away from the fireball and out of the sandy whirlwind. Emily saw Raquel had taken her place in holding the fireball.

"And here's Knight and Martin - God knows what's going on in there - but - Martin's flown back inside the whirlwind leaving Knight alone but where's Kena?" Harmony questioned.

A breathless Emily helplessly watched the whirlwind swallow up her team mates. The crowd were eerily silent as they watched in a trance-like state, the sand gathering from the floor and entwining with the whirlwind, which now dominated the centre of the stadium.

Emily flew up towards the sky, a few metres above the whirlwind to find a dirty and torn Julian Kena, looking horrified at what he had helped to create. Yellow, grainy specks stood out in his silky, black hair. He glanced at Emily and caught her eye, both aware that the match was far from over but too transfixed to care.

"This match has taken a different route to how it began, even Kena and Knight have stopped their battle and are watching. I can't see a thing - what about you, Wesley?" Harmony asked.

"Bloody nothing! We'll just have to wait."

They didn't have to wait long. The whirlwind was slowly beginning to turn different colours, for a second it would be a deep blue and then a vibrant red but then it began to turn yellow, so bright that it was almost white. Emily shielded her eyes as the light got bigger and brighter. BANG!

The force of the fireball exploding blew Emily and Julian back several metres. Emily yelled as sand roughly hit her face. She waited a few seconds and slowly opened her eyes. She looked down and saw that the light from the fireball was gone and Raquel and Rosa were sprawled out over the sandy floor. Lee-Smith and Edge were flying around them, moving a lot slower, and when Ferguson examined Rosa and Raquel, he nodded at Lee-Smith and Edge and waved two blue flags.

Emily had never heard a stadium cheer as loudly as she did then. It was so loud that she couldn't hear Wesley and Harmony commentate on their microphones. An eruption of blue flags and fans chanting 'Mentorawth' echoed around Emily and that's when she realised that Lee-Smith, Edge and Kena had surrounded her in a triangle formation.

Emily tried desperately to think of a plan as she looked from one pair of eyes to the other but she had nothing. She flew up, they followed her. She flew to the left and to the right and they were still there in their triangle formation. Sylvia Lee-Smith threw a punch at her face. Emily caught her fist and twisted Sylvia's arm round to her back. Jansi Edge went to kick her. Emily caught her foot and threw it away from her. Julian shot a fireball. Emily turned Sylvia round so she would get hit but Sylvia managed to get out of Emily's grip and ducked, which forced Emily to duck also. Before Emily knew it, she was dodging in and out of their attacks, restraining herself not to hit the Distracters.

"There's no way she can win this!" Harmony said. "Come on Wesley, three against one!"

"Shut up, Harmony! I'm trying to think," Wesley snapped.

Emily had been hit four times in the mouth and was bleeding heavily. Julian Kena punched her hard in her lower back and Emily screamed in agony.

"Knight doesn't look too good and the odds don't look too hopeful," Harmony said, glancing at Wesley, who's expression was blank. "Kena's grabbed her in a bear hug! Squeezing the poor girl's torso and I can only imagine the pain."

Emily wanted it all to end. She was exhausted and drenched in her own blood. Her body was aching all over, she could barely hold herself up.

"Looks like Mentorawth's going to take this one, I think -" but before Harmony had finished her sentence, Wesley grabbed the microphone off her.

"Emily you're so useless! Come on you lazy git, you're meant to be Thomas Knights daughter!"

"Wesley, what are you doing?" Harmony asked outraged. "Give it back!"

Wesley pushed Harmony's arm away as the audience watched bemused.

"Look at her, what a bloody joke. She's nothing like her dad - she's just an embarrassment! You're only good for being on the front of papers for your thieving. You haven't got any skills."

The audience gasped as Emily's head turned. She couldn't believe her ears. Why was Wesley insulting her? Even the Mentorawth Distracters were looking at him; Julian had loosened his grip with his mouth hanging open in disbelief.

"She's getting annoyed. Our new hero? You were right Ems, they really were taking the piss!"

"Shut up," Emily said, closing her eyes. She could feel her anger slowly rising.

"Loser, you're a loser," Wesley sang over the microphone.

"Shut up," Emily said again, clenching her fists. She was breathing hard.

"Everyone join in - loser!"

She looked around at all the faces laughing at her with hatred in her eyes.

"SHUT UP!" Emily roared.

The stadium disappeared into a stunning, white light. Julian Kena, Sylvia Lee-Smith and Jansi Edge attempted to push back her huge, powerful fireball but they didn't succeed as they were knocked back by its power. The protective glass that covered the audience smashed into little pieces. Sylvia, Jansi and Julian were motionless on the sandy floor. Students and teachers were screaming and staring at Emily horrified. Some were running out of the stadium. Harmony ducked under the commentators' table. Emily hovered in the middle of the stadium with her ears ringing, her eyes wet but transfixed on one person. Wesley stared back at her, grinning from ear to ear.

Emily awoke to see fields of snow across her garden and Rosy, Yvonne and James laughing as they made snowmen and snow angels. The Christmas Holidays were approaching fast and Emily couldn't contain her excitement. She was even looking forward to the burnt, inedible mess, Sally passed off as Christmas dinner. But she was especially looking forward to meeting Michella's family as Michella had asked Emily to come over during the holidays.

The whole school was buzzing from the match, stopping Emily to tell her how amazing she was. Julian Kena, Sylvia Lee-Smith and Jansi Edge had spent three weeks in the sick bay and were forced to drink Reviving Water every hour, so that they could be fully healed. Julian was now sporting a faint bruise on his cheek and he was the only Mentorawth student who congratulated Emily on winning. The Ogragons were ecstatic and Lenny couldn't stop hugging her but there was one Ogragon who's congratulations Emily didn't want to hear.

Wesley had taken to leaving the Ogragon living room when Emily came in and Emily was grateful. Since the match, she had refused to speak to him and shouted at him when he attempted to explain himself. In Emily's books, their friendship was over.

"You know you're welcome round mine too during the Christmas holidays. I'm only around the corner from Michella's," Jason said to her during dinner. "My parents would love to meet you."

"Thanks Jas," Emily replied. She smiled to herself as she thought of the girls in her dorm and how they would hate her if she went to Jason's house.

"And Wesley as well - he'd also like it -"

"I'd rather battle Neci," Emily interrupted as Michella and Jason looked at each other.

I AM...

"That's a bit of an exaggeration," Michella exclaimed. "You don't mean that."

"I do," Emily said glancing at Wesley, who was seated at the far end of the table next to Pete and Warren. He hadn't touched his plate.

They ate their food in silence. Emily knew that Jason and Michella didn't understand why she was so angry with Wesley but she didn't understand how they couldn't. How did they expect her to forgive Wesley when he had shouted out her insecurities in front of the entire school? On loud speaker! In her eyes that was unforgivable.

"Knight!"

Emily jumped and looked around to see Ms Macay walking towards her.

"The headmaster would like to see you in his office."

Emily had enough experience to last her a lifetime with angry head teachers.

"Me?" Emily squeaked. "Why?"

Ms Macay shrugged her shoulders, "He would like you to go now. Take the left corridor, then another left until you see a door with a cross on it. The pin is 060888. He will join you shortly."

Ms Macay walked off and Emily said goodbye to Jason and Michella and left the dining table. It didn't take her long to find Mr Davon's office. Emily was typing in the pin when she felt a strong hand on her shoulder.

"We need to talk," Wesley said boldly.

"I don't have time for this," Emily snapped, brushing him off.

"I was trying to help! Ever since the Baby Ball and in the stadium, I realised -"

"Aah," Emily grunted. "You made me mess up the pin. Just go away!"

"Emily please -"

"Haven't you said enough? Our friendship ended as soon as you spoke on that microphone," Emily shouted at him.

"Is there a problem here?" a deep voice called down the corridor.

The pair turned to find Mr Davon walking towards them in his black training kit. He stared from one to the other with a slight crease in his forehead.

"No sir, Wesley was just leaving," Emily said, staring at Wesley, daring him to question her. Wesley didn't say a word but he diverted his eyes away from Emily towards Mr Davon and Emily was sure that she saw Mr Davon ever so slightly nod his head.

"Good," Mr Davon said. "Emily kindly wait for me in my office."

He pressed in the pin number and held open the door for her. Emily walked slowly towards it, glancing back at Wesley, who was still not looking at her. Mr Davon smiled warmly at Emily before closing the door. She pressed her ear up against the cool oak doors, desperate to hear but she couldn't hear a thing. Slightly annoyed, she walked up the stairs to Mr Davon's office.

'Mr Davon - Headmaster' shone in gold lettering and Emily gently traced it with her finger before she went inside the office. She stopped and looked around with her eyes wide and her mouth hanging open, trying to take it in all at once.

A rainbow of training kits hung on the right side of the room. On the left side of the room was a painting from the floor to the ceiling of a famous warrior picture. It was of the leaders of the Warrior Revolution. Ordinary warriors that did extraordinary things. Bernard Ogragon was a short, stocky man with thick, blonde hair and a comely face. Joseph Berbinin was Indian. He had a chubby, friendly face and a receding hairline. Idris Jenkint had tribal markings tattooed on his face. He was thin and dark skinned. Arthur Linktie was a tall, lean, olive skinned man. His face was very hard and sculptured. Rose-Marie Mentorawth was a middle aged woman with a blonde bob, who wore small, square shaped glasses and lastly Ce-Ce Pentwon, with her black hair in twists. She was the youngest one in the group and she was showing of her enviable stomach and heaving bosom.

They were firing huge fireballs at a thousand man army of uncontrollable warriors who were charging at them. Emily noticed how the warriors were drawn with sunken faces, bloodshot eyes and ripped clothing while the leaders stood over them, graceful and beautiful, defeating them effortlessly.

Emily closed the door and gasped when she saw a photograph of the Five Warriors. This one she had never seen before although they hadn't changed much. They were all in Osaki uniforms apart from Cecil. Cecil was stood kneeling over and laughing. His thick blonde hair, hung loose over his shoulders. Jenkins was a slim, tall teenager who had the most handsome face. He had short afro hair and was looking up at a very young Niles and laughing. Niles's baby face was animated as he stared at Jenkins. He looked like he was explaining a humorous story. Jenkins was holding the beautiful Italian, Roberta's hand. Roberta had thick, black wavy hair and full lips. She was smiling directly at the camera. Mr Davon looked the same except he had less wrinkles and blonde hair and the man with his arms around Mr Davon's shoulders was Thomas Knight.

Emily reached out her hand slowly and gently touched the face of her father. She was taking in every last detail from his curly dark hair and his cheeky, dimpled smile to his dark, fitted training kit that showed off his toned, statue like stance. The face she had not seen since she was seven but yet graced the cover of every book, magazine and newspaper. Everyone wanted a piece of Thomas Knight and the one that needed it the most didn't get a share.

Mesmerized by the photo she didn't notice Mr Davon teleport into the office. He watched her silently admiring her father's picture.

"I remember that day very well."

Emily jumped but smiled when she saw the headmaster, "When was this taken?"

Mr Davon frowned in concentration, "Around eighteen years ago in the school grounds. Thomas, Roberta and Jenkins would have been about sixteen, Niles was thirteen and Cecil was mid fifties."

Lox looked just like Thomas. Emily shook her head in an attempt to rid the images of her brother's sunken face and the desperate look in his eyes. Emily turned away from the picture. Staring at her Dad and remembering Lox wasn't helpful. Mr Davon motioned for her to take a seat. She sat opposite him and he rested his chin on his clasped hands.

"Well done for your win against Mentorawth, that was a spectacular fight."

"Thank you, sir," Emily replied humbly.

"But I did have some concerns, I would like to share with you."

"Oh," Emily said, surprised of the seriousness in his tone.

"From watching your match Emily and speaking to Cecil and Niles, I realised that you are not very aware of your powers."

Emily frowned, "I don't understand."

"What I mean Emily, is you find it difficult to produce a Baby Ball which is very basic, something I expect all of my students to do within the first month of joining the school but yet in the match, you managed to produce a magnificent fireball at the same level as any advanced warrior could. This baffled me greatly but after speaking to Wesley minutes ago, my fear was confirmed."

"Wesley!" Emily said surprised. "What did he say? What fear?"

Mr Davon held up his hand. Embarrassed by her reaction, Emily fell silent.

"During Cecil and Niles's class, you couldn't produce a Baby Ball on demand and before Wesley made his announcement, you were fighting . . . okay. You were doing well but you hadn't shot a single fireball. But when Wesley spoke on the microphone and you got angry, I sensed a power far higher than before. Your energy level soared, you were untouchable. Only then did you produce a fireball."

Mr Davon got up and began to pace around his office. He was frowning as he stared into space. Emily's eyes followed him.

"Wesley noticed the same things. He saw you one night in the stadium, practising by yourself before the match. He was in the commentators' box and he watched you. He sensed your power rise tremendously when you got angry and only then could you produce your fireball."

Emily remembered before the match, she was angry about Lox and she saw the figure in the commentators' box. She had no idea it was Wesley.

"Also at the Revolution Night party, I was told from witnesses that you shot a fireball at the intruder. I'm guessing you were scared?" Mr Davon raised an eyebrow and Emily reluctantly nodded.

"I'm also assuming this has happened before?"

Emily nodded, remembering the lady in the shop who had accused her of stealing and the fire that had appeared in her hand. She had never created fire before or since then.

"Do you see it Emily?" Mr Davon said, turning to her. "Your powers are controlled by your emotions. When you're happy or nervous you can perform at a standard level but when you're petrified or rage comes over you, your powers are unlimited. This is dangerous for any warrior Emily but especially you."

Emily shrugged her shoulders, "I know at times my power has a mind of its own and it's not convenient and sometimes it gets me into more trouble than needed but during the match, my emotions really saved my butt."

Mr Davon shook his head, "You misunderstand me. Ordinary people do crazy things when their emotions run wild. Now imagine a warrior but a warrior with unlimited power who can't control their emotions. If Julian had managed to still battle after that humongous fireball, your rage would have increased and you probably could have killed him or possibly yourself."

Emily gasped and covered her mouth. She shook her head vigorously, "But I wouldn't have, I've never killed -".

"You could have," he said, sitting back in his seat. He stared at her solemnly. "A good fighter knows how to control their power and increase it at their demand. Emily, you need to learn to control your emotions especially your rage because it can be deadly to those whom you truly care for."

Emily shook her head in disbelief, "I can't believe . . . I mean I wouldn't kill . . . Wesley clocked all of this? Why didn't he tell me? Man, I've been such a cow to him."

Mr Davon laughed, "He wanted to be certain. During the match Emily, Wesley saw you were out of your depth. You were in a desperate situation so he did a desperate thing. I'm not saying he did it in the best way but there's no denying it was done out of love. Offence is expensive. Think about friendships you'll lose because you got offended."

Mr Davon smiled, "Don't fight your friends, Emily especially a good one like Wesley."

Emily nodded, feeling ashamed of herself. Her head was buzzing. She put her fingers to her temple and massaged them. Mr Davon looked at his watch.

"I do apologise for making you miss the rest of dinner, this was the only time I had to speak. You're free to go but please for your own good, think about what I said."

Emily nodded again, "Thanks sir, for warning me."

"That's what I'm here for," he said kindly.

As soon as she left the office, Emily ran up to the Ogragon living room, praying that Wesley was there. He was sitting on the couch with Michella and Jason. They were laughing at something but when he saw Emily, he abruptly stopped. Michella and Jason looked from Emily to Wesley. Embarrassed but determined, Emily walked up to a nervous

Wesley and threw her arms around him in the tightest hug she could master.

"What? I don't -" he started.

Emily pulled away from him, "I'm sorry for not hearing you out and for ever doubting you would do anything to hurt me. You were just being a good friend."

Wesley slowly smiled and hugged Emily back, pulling her on top of him so they both toppled over the chair and on to the floor. Michella and Jason laughed.

"Finally!" Michella said. "This was starting to get really awkward."

"Starting to?" Jason raised his eyebrows. "I was making a mental timetable in my head, making sure I spent equal time with the both of them. Monday was Emily, Tuesday was Wesley, Wednesday was Emily -"

"Alright, alright we get it," Emily said laughing. "I'm glad we're cool again."

"Me too," Wesley said. "These two are rubbish at playing card games. Winning's been too easy!"

"Whatever," Michella said, throwing her pillow at him, which knocked his hat off his head making them all laugh and Emily silently vowed to herself to never doubt her friends again.

CHAPTER NINE

A Dark Christmas

Christmas was around the corner and Emily, Michella, Wesley and Jason were covered in snow as they trooped to their last History lesson before the holidays.

"I never was one for the manufactured Christmas that the Government has tricked us into believing is traditional," Mr King said, looking down in disgust at Violet Hijen and Sydney John because they were wearing gold tinsel in their hair and reindeer hair bands.

"I mean the real celebration of Christmas is the birth of Jesus," Mr King drawled. "Yet everyone and anyone celebrates it. I mean does everyone celebrate Eid? Or Passover? Or -"

"Sir," Michella said, putting her hand up. "Are you religious? Because just last week you said you were flying to Vegas to get drunk and meet lots of show girls."

Mr King flared his nostrils as the class laughed, "I think the real question Miss Kinkle is are you religious? Seeing as you sit there every week questioning what I say!"

Michella laughed, "Sir, that's not exactly a commandment."

"Well, it should be," Mr King said, narrowing his eyes.

He looked at Michella's school bag, which was an unattractive swirl of orange and brown. Mr King shuddered and wrinkled his nose in disgust,

I AM . . .

"Be careful, Miss Kinkle, HE does see all." And he walked away with his nose turned up.

Flying was outside in the snow and Emily stood shivering in her thin training kit. Tanya had attempted to wear her gloves and they were now on the floor by Ms Macay's feet.

"They cost me a tenner and she just put them on the snow!" Emily over heard Tanya, who was standing behind her, hiss to Ola.

"And now they're wet," Emily said, turning round and smiling at Tanya.

"Careful Emily, it'll be your head sticking out of the snow," Tanya threatened and Emily laughed.

"Okay class," Ms Macay said, rubbing her hands together. "I know it's absolutely freezing and that's why we're going to work on controlling our speed with flying."

The class cheered loudly. Emily was open to anything that would get her warm.

"The hardest part is learning how to accelerate as you fly. The technique is pretty easy but trust me, it can get a bit scary when you're zooming past everything so quick. Yes Tanya?"

Tanya put her hand down and boldly asked, "Miss can you please take my gloves off the floor? I paid a tenner for them and now they're going to be wet and gross."

"£10 for gloves?" Wesley hollered over the class's laughter. "The same ones are a £1 in the market."

Tanya rolled her eyes, "Well they're obviously better than a pound gloves. It's just a question of standards Wesley. We can all see how low yours are."

"Hey!" Ms Macay shouted as Wesley opened his mouth to retaliate. "Knock it off, the pair off you. Tanya you brought gloves to the lesson knowing that you shouldn't so deal with it being gross okay?"

Tanya pouted and everyone laughed.

"Guys quiet down," Ms Macay shouted. "Now, it's scary when you're flying really fast. So to increase your speed, you have to make sure your body's rigid with your arms stuck to your body and your legs stuck together. Imagine if you were lying on the floor, your body would be flat. That's the same position you'll be but standing up. Jason come here a sec."

Jason walked to Ms Macay. His blonde hair was blowing wildly in the wind.

"Right can you lift up from the floor so your knees are about this height?" Ms Macay said. She held her arm out straight.

"Sure."

Jason bent his knees and flew up a few centimetres so his knees were at Ms Macay's shoulder level. Ms Macay bent down, grabbed his legs and pulled them up towards her, so that Jason's body was straight as if he was lying on something. The wind blew up Jason's top revealing a toned torso to the delight of all the girls.

"Mmmm, that is lovely," Lisa Fowler drooled.

"This is the position everyone needs to be in in the air and your body needs to stay tense. Let's all try it."

The class spent most of the lesson practising the technique. Emily found it weird lying so rigid in the air. She was used to flying with her arms all over the place and her body feeling relaxed. When Ms Macay was satisfied with their techniques, she made them fly slowly around the stadium in that position and then they had to gradually speed up at her command.

"Seeing as it's only half a day today and you guys are leaving in a few hours, let's have some fun. Jenkint verses Ogragon verses Linktie. We'll see which is the fastest team to fly around the stadium."

Everyone cheered.

"What do we win?" Harmony Loving-Dale asked. Her blonde hair was plaited into small individual plaits with shells in them.

I AM...

Ms Macay grinned, "The winning team gets a hamper of chocolates from Macnocs after the holidays and just so you know the Ogragon team hold the title with three seconds! Okay enough chat, let's race."

The holidays had officially begun and Emily was seated in the back seat of the Kinkle's family car with Michella, Pete, Warren and Lenny. Mrs Kinkle was a chubby lady with shoulder length, glossy black hair and a diamond nose piercing. She was driving and muttering about "Stupid London and its damn weather."

Sally and Mrs Kinkle had agreed that Emily would stay for a couple of days over the holidays and Mrs Kinkle would drive her home before Christmas. On the phone, Sally had told Emily that she had posted on an early Christmas present to the Kinkle's house. She said it was very special and she wanted Emily to open it as soon as she could.

As they drove up the gravel driveway to Michella's house all Emily could say was "Wow." In front of her stood a grand, four storey, white bricked house, covered head to toe in Christmas decorations and a massive neon sign flashing 'Merry Christmas.'

"It's very bright," Emily said.

Michella laughed, "We do tacky the best. Wesley and Jason live up the road, they tried to pull all this off." Michella pointed at the lights, "But we put theirs to shame."

"I've got your bag, Emily," Lenny said, holding his rucksack in one hand and Emily's suitcase in the other.

"Thanks Lenny," Emily said gratefully, as she followed him and Michella into the house. They led her to the kitchen. Even though Michella's family was around the same size as Emily's, their kitchen was the tidiest, cleanest kitchen she had ever seen. Everything seemed to sparkle, even the cutlery was put away in height order. Emily hadn't seen her house that clean since the housekeeper was let go. Emily took a seat at the glistening kitchen counter, when the door swung open.

"You're back!" a young boy and girl screamed in unison as they ran to Michella squeezing her in a big hug.

"I missed you guys. How was the show?"

"Amazing," the boy said. He had shoulder length plaits and almond shaped brown eyes. "I hit one note wrong though but the judges didn't seem to care because I won!"

"Well done, Mike!" Lenny said, from next to the fridge. The boy ran up to him and gave him a high five.

"What about you Madi?"

Madison, a beautiful girl with the thickest, longest eyelashes, Emily had ever seen, shrugged her shoulders looking slightly bored, "Oh you know, the same old thing. Went to some casting jobs with Mum and Macnocs are interested in using me for their adverts." She smiled gleefully.

"What's this about Macnocs?" Pete asked, as he entered the kitchen with Warren behind him.

"They may use me to advertise their products," Madison sang.

"Seriously?" Pete asked stunned.

"All those free sweets," Warren said dreamily. "You know you've always been my favourite sister."

"Hey!" Michella said, frowning at him.

"Sorry, I mean my fav little sister."

"Warren!"

"Oh, I can't win can I?" Warren said dramatically, throwing his arms up in the air.

Michella shook her head. She looked at Emily as if just remembering she was there.

"Mike, Madison, this is my friend Emily Knight. Emily, my little brother and sister, Mike and Madison."

The pair looked at each other and Emily watched Mike nod at Madison and Madison pull out a crumpled piece of paper, which she looked at, then at Emily, then back again at her paper.

"What are you doing?" Michella asked, confused.

"I'm just making sure," Madison looked up from the paper to look at Emily again. "That it's really her."

"What?" Michella asked as Emily and her brothers snickered. "What did you think I was lying?"

"Yes," they replied, without a moment's hesitation.

"Oh, get out of here!" Michella snapped.

"How many times do you really need to watch that school musical film, Madi?" Mrs Kinkle sighed, as they were all seated in the living room and the table was covered with bowls of popcorn.

"It's really good - oh, shut up Warren," Madison snapped when he laughed. "It's better than *The Don*."

Warren, Pete and Lenny gasped.

"How can you even put the two in the same sentence?" Pete asked horrified. "Where's Mike? Let's see what he picks."

"I'll get him," Emily offered, as the boys and Madison hounded Michella to pick the best film.

Emily walked down the corridor towards Mike's room, when she heard soft classical music coming from the door at the end of the corridor. Emily ran towards it and watched Mike playing the black piano in the music room. His fingers moved delicately over the keys creating a beautiful melody, mesmerizing Emily. Emily swayed her head to the rhythm and when Mike stopped, she applauded him, making him jump.

"Sorry," Emily said guiltily. "That was so good! How old are you again?"

"I'm almost eight," Mike said looking away shyly. "Err . . . you can play on it, I was only messing about."

"I couldn't play after that!" Emily said smiling. "You're a very talented guy."

Mike bowed his head humbly, "Thank you."

"MIKE, EMILY - WHO THE BLODDY HELL'S THAT!" Pete cried irritably, as the doorbell cut him mid sentence.

"Well, it can't be your Dad," Mrs Kinkle said thoughtfully. "He's not back from his business trip till tomorrow."

Emily and Mike walked down the corridor together as Pete answered the door. A tall woman wrapped in a grey jacket and matching scarf was holding a large suitcase. Her curly auburn hair rested neatly on her shoulders and she smiled at Pete, which lit up her pretty face.

"Peter!" the lady screamed. She dropped her luggage on the floor and threw her arms around him. "I haven't seen you in forever!"

Pete laughed, "The match was amazing, I didn't know you got another one."

"Yeah, a while back."

She released him and clasped eyes on Mike. She screamed Mike's name and devoured him in a tight hug as Emily watched on. The rest of the Kinkle's came trooping out of the living room looking puzzled but they all broke into huge smiles, shouting, "Welcome home, Janette."

Emily watched as the family embraced Janette, kissing and laughing with her until Janette's eyes fell on Emily and she approached her.

"Hello there," Janette said, shaking Emily's hand. She narrowed her eyes, "You look really familiar."

I AM . . .

"I'm Emily Knight."

Janette took a step back. She looked back at her family in amazement, "Are you serious? As in Thomas Knight's daughter?"

"That's me," Emily said, laughing at the shock on Janette's face.

"Wow, it's an honour to have you in our house, Emily. Please excuse the massacre outside the house or what they like to call, Christmas decorations. Do you know your father was the sole reason why I wanted to play professional Dojo? The man's amazing."

Emily's ears perked up, "Oh yeah, you play for the London Flyaways and England?"

Janette nodded, "Do you play at school?"

Emily nodded happily, "Yeah, I play for Ogragon and I'm their fifth fighter."

"She's so good," Michella chipped in.

"That's easy to believe," Janette said, smiling at Emily. "You lot won any matches?"

"Yep, we beat Mentorawth. Lenny's a great captain."

"Lenny? Captain? Oh bless him," Janette teased, pulling on his cheeks.

"Shut up," Lenny snapped and he hit her hands away from his face.

They followed Janette to the living room except for Mrs Kinkle who went to dish out the dinner and all of the Kinkle kids circled around her as she sat on an armchair. Michella beckoned for Emily to join them and she did, confused as to what they were looking for.

"Let's see it then," Michella whispered.

"See what?" Janette frowned.

Madison tutted, "The tattoo of course. Quick before Mum comes."

Janette looked at them all and sighed loudly even though she was enjoying the attention. She stood up, removed her coat and turned her back on them. She lifted up her green cashmere jumper and they all gasped.

"You like?" she called to them.

In the middle of her back was a large eagle, with its wings outstretched. Every detail was etched into her glowing black skin, from the feathers which were individually different, to the glint in the birds eye and the mountains and waterfall in the background. The tattoo was breathtaking. The best artwork Emily had ever seen.

"Amazing," Emily muttered to herself.

"That's what the captain for Germany said," Janette boasted. "He was in complete awe, that's how I managed to hit him with a fireball right in his face. He was well pissed off."

The living room door opened and everyone jumped as Janette pulled down her jumper and instantly resumed her position on the armchair. Mrs Kinkle was at the doorway with her apron on, not noticing the plastered smiles on Emily and her children's faces in a bid to look natural.

"Dinner's ready."

That night as the household slept, a figure in black teleported into the Kinkle's household. Scared yet determined to do what it was set out to do, the figure stood silently, listening to the gentle snores of the family up above, wishing that time could go back to when life was less complicated.

The black figure moved towards the stairs but stopped. She was definitely here but there were too many powerful warriors present who would protect her. The black figure crept silently into the living room and looked around. Typical, it thought. The decorated tree which was placed next to the window, to show off to the neighbours and the stacks of presents that were under it.

The figure knelt next to the tree and fingered a square shaped present wrapped in gold, labelled 'Emily.' The figure ripped it open to find a picture of Thomas and Leah Knight standing side by side. Thomas had a protective arm over a young Lox, one of the few photographs where Lox smiled. Leah, a beautiful, young woman with her light brown eyes, that shone with happiness as she looked down adoringly at little Emily, who she was holding in her arms. Leah's black hair hung loose and Emily's little hand was reaching up to grab it. The black figure turned it over and found a note reading 'I will see you soon. I love you' signed from Thomas Knight.

The black figure turned the frame over again and stared silently at the picture and put its index finger in the middle of it and the picture began to melt and shrivel up. The figure threw it carelessly on to the floor and looked angrily at all of the presents, picking them up one by one and throwing them, breaking them all. The figure cried out and kicked the decorated tree over. *Why was everything so hard?* The black figure wanted to stick to the plan and take her from her bed but it couldn't do it, at least not today. So when the figure heard someone stirring upstairs, it fled.

Upstairs, Emily was tossing and muttering in her sleep. Her dad was hugging her mother and Lox was stomping up the stairs, looking back at his father with hatred. Lox was in front of her, now older and he was smiling at her. Emily reached out to him but she couldn't touch him. The more she tried, the further away he went until he was gone.

"No," Emily muttered sleepily. "Lox, no."

Mrs Kinkle trooped down the stairs half asleep, convinced she hadn't seasoned the turkey yet, even though she had. She walked past the living room and then walked back to it. She knew she had closed the door but the living room door was wide open. She turned on the lights and screamed when she saw the broken and burnt mess on the floor.

Lights turned on throughout the house and panicked voices soon followed. Emily sat straight up in her bed, her brow wet and when she heard the voices, she jumped up and raced down the stairs. She found a distraught Mrs Kinkle huddled on the floor, in front of the tree, crying.

"Oh, no," Madison said, dropping to her knees when she saw the mess.

Janette and Michella ran over to comfort their mother, while Warren ran outside to see if he could see anyone. Lenny ordered Pete and Madison to help clean up the mess as Emily hugged Mike tight, who was holding in his tears. They all looked in horror at the mess.

"Who would do such a thing?" Mrs Kinkle cried. "And on Christmas? What monster would . . ."

She trailed off as the tears overcame her.

"If I ever catch that git," Warren said angrily, storming back into the house and throwing the pieces of glass into the rubbish bin Lenny had provided.

Emily got on her hands and knees to help as well and she picked up the burnt picture on the floor. She stared at it hard but she couldn't make out what it was. It was covered in black, so unaware, she threw her father's present into the bin.

CHAPTER TEN

Ogragon vs Linktie

Mrs Kinkle called her husband to inform him of recent events and reassuring him that he didn't have to rush home from his business trip in New York. Then she called Sally and Michael and Janette drove Emily home. They spoke light heartedly about Dojo and Emily got advice on creating Baby Balls and standard fireballs. They both avoided the subject of the break-in throughout the journey.

When Janette pulled up at the house, Sally and Michael were waiting outside in their housecoats and slippers, hugging themselves because of the cold. As soon as Emily got out of the car, they grabbed her and held her tight.

"Mrs Kinkle called us about the break-in. I thought something had happened to you," Michael said. He kissed Emily's forehead.

"I would never have forgiven myself," Sally said distraught.

Emily could feel them both shaking.

"I'd better get a move on, Mum's a mess," Janette said, shaking Michael and Sally's hands.

"Thank you for driving her home," Michael said.

"No problem and Emily make sure you practise the techniques we discussed and you'll be fine." Janette winked at her before she got back in the car and drove off.

The three of them entered the house. Emily breathed in the familiar smell of home and she took off her many layers as is was too hot inside. The Christmas tree was messily decorated by the kids and there were stacks of presents underneath it. Tinsel and Christmas cards were hung everywhere and a banner that Emily could just about read said 'Merry Christmas' in Yvonne's messy writing.

Emily sat at the dining table. Sally sat opposite her and stared at her.

"I'm fine, Sally chill out."

Sally shook her head, "Do you think it was a coincidence that someone broke into the Kinkle's house while you were there?"

Emily shrugged, "Well it must have been. No one knew I was going and remember Janette is some big international star. It was probably some crazy fan, that's what Janette thinks too."

Sally sighed deeply, "You didn't open the present I told you to open did you?"

Emily frowned, then gasped when she remembered, "Oh no I forgot and now it's gone. What was it?"

"It was a present from your Dad. A family picture. I knew how happy you would be so I sent it on."

"The burnt picture?"

Sally raised her eyebrows, "Mrs Kinkle said it was the only present that was burnt. Why?"

Emily stayed silent and looked at the Christmas tree in the living room. *Why would someone come all the way to Michella's house and not attack anyone? Why was my present the only one destroyed?*

"I don't know," Emily said quietly.

She looked up and saw tears falling down Sally's pale face, "I'm scared for you, Emily."

She reached out her hand across the table and Emily held on to it and Sally collapsed on the table and cried.

I AM . . .

Emily spent the rest of Christmas Day with a plastered smile, playing every game possible with James, Rosy and Yvonne and gossiping with Cathy about the boys at school.

"You so do like Wesley!" Cathy squealed at the dinner table, over the turkey.

"Sssh," Emily snapped, when everyone looked at them.

"You do," Cathy whispered. "And Julian too. Look at you Ems, regular little minx!"

"I haven't done anything," Emily hissed.

"Not yet," Cathy sang.

Emily, Sally and Michael had agreed to keep the break-in away from the others. It didn't help that the phone rang constantly on Boxing Day. When it rang for what seemed like the hundredth time, Emily screamed in frustration, picked up the ringing phone and barked, "What?"

"Hello, is it true that there was a break-in at Janette Kinkle's house and Emily Knight was in the house and -"

"No comment," Emily said and she slammed the phone down.

It didn't take long for the paparazzi to camp outside their house and ring the doorbell, so they spent the rest of the Christmas holidays indoors with the curtains closed. Sally was so worried about Emily, that she made her have a phone counselling session with Jenny. Emily found the session pointless. She didn't know how she felt or why this was happening to her, so how could she explain it to somebody else?

Emily used the time she was stuck indoors to practise Janette's technique. She practised at every opportunity on how to focus her energy until she could produce Baby Balls and standard fireballs effortlessly.

Emily couldn't wait to go back to school. She was sick of being stuck indoors and she missed Michella, Wesley and Jason. It wasn't turning out to be the Christmas she had imagined.

On the journey back to school, the paparazzi followed Sally's car all the way to St Bertudes Bus Station, shoving people out of the way and asking Emily about the break-in. She replied, "No comment" but it fell on deaf ears and they continued to take endless pictures of her. Emily was thankful for security who escorted them back outside the bus station.

Throughout the first week at school, students and teachers approached Emily and the Kinkles to share their sympathies with them. It was a Friday afternoon and Emily had just finished her Water Studies lesson, where she was now one of a few people who still couldn't breathe under water. Wesley had just started a new game of cards and was dealing her and Jason in. Emily was smiling at the great hand she had been dealt, when Michella ran into the living room, waving the Daily Steward and at the same time Lenny approached Emily.

"Ready for the match, champ?"

Emily nodded, "As ready as I'm ever going to be. A bit nervous though."

"Nervous?" Lenny shouted, making everyone look over at them. "Just do what you did against that Julian kid and we'll do great. See you in the changing room for three."

"I think he meant don't do what you did against Julian. Keep your emotions under control remember?" Jason said.

"As long as Wesley doesn't get the audience singing loser at me, I think I'll be fine," Emily teased. She nudged Wesley.

Wesley laughed, "I've learnt my lesson."

Lenny walked towards the living room door only stopping to talk to Michella, who showed him something in the paper and he hurried out of the door.

"What was that about?" Jason asked, flicking his golden hair out of his face.

"We're in the paper again. The latest version of the story," Michella said. She looked anxious.

"Great," Emily said throwing her jacks and twos on the floor. "Let's have a read."

Michella opened the paper to page six.

KNIGHT'S CHRISTMAS DAY BREAK-IN!
By
Alice Kite

A break-in took place at the home of Janette Kinkle, 24, the heavily tattooed Distracter for England's household on Christmas Day. It is believed that the person broke in while the family were asleep and destroyed their Christmas decorations and presents.

Emily Knight, 13, daughter of The Five Warriors legend Thomas Knight, was in the household staying with the family and was said to be "upset and confused about the motives." In particular a family photo from her father was burnt during the break-in.

This is just another blow to Emily whose mother, Leah Knight, died at the age of 33 from breast cancer and whose brother, Lox Knight, is believed to have been kidnapped at aged 13. Millions of pounds have been donated for his return. Police are still investigating.

Jason closed the paper and laughed, "Don't you find it amazing how they turned the break-in, into the Knight's family history?"

Emily scrunched the newspaper into a ball and threw it into the bin opposite her, "How useless are they? This happened on Christmas Eve! I didn't even say any of that and Lox wasn't kidnapped and how the hell did they know about my Dad's present?"

"They probably tapped your phone line," Wesley said.

Michella had a far away look in her eyes and it took Jason's nudge for her to snap back.

"Sorry," Michella said, shaking her head. "I was just thinking whether the break-in and the Revolution Night attack could be connected."

The three of them looked at her.

Emily frowned, "Why would they be?"

"I don't know," Michella said carefully. "It's just that at the Revolution Night party, you were attacked." She looked at Emily, "And then my house is broken into and they burn your photo -"

"Man, you sound like Sally. I know how it sounds but it doesn't mean it's connected," Emily cut in, not liking what Michella was implying.

"I know, I know," Michella said frowning. "But it's likely and you being who you are, you're sort of . . . well . . . a target."

Wesley and Jason stared at Michella as Emily let out a nervous laugh.

"A target? Come on now, Mich, that's a bit extreme. Who would be after me?" But Emily remembered Lox saying that she wasn't safe. *Is this what Lox meant?*

"Is it extreme though?" Michella asked seriously. "It's just a bit weird. I don't know, I just think we've got to keep our eyes open. Just in case. Yes!"

Michella put down a Black Jack on top of the Red Jack.

"Pick up five, Emily," Wesley instructed but Emily's drive to compete was gone.

Three o' clock struck as Emily entered the changing room and the rest of the Ogragons were already in their crimson coloured uniform. Emily slipped hers on as Lenny began to pace around the changing room.

"Okay, team," Lenny said. "This is it. If we win this match we overtake Linktie and we'll face Pentwon for the cup. Fight your hardest, fight your best and let's win this."

I AM . . .

He put his hand out and everyone piled their hands on top of his and yelled, "Ogragon." Lenny led his team to the pitch with Harmony Loving-Dale screaming out their names, "Lenny Kinkle, Summer Wind, Raquel Davis, Rosa Martin, Pete Kinkle, Warren Kinkle and Emily Knight!"

The crowd were cheering loudly. Ogragon faced Linktie who stood in front of them in black training kits. Emily wished Tanya was playing. She wasn't allowed to because Jessi Kendaschi wasn't fighting and they had to have an even number of fighters. Emily would have loved an excuse to punch Tanya and not get into trouble for it.

"And they're off," Wesley bellowed into the microphone. "The captains, Lenny Kinkle from Ogragon and Josie Harrington from Linktie start off the match. Harrington's blows are making a slight impact on Kinkle's usual standard of performance but Kinkle's got speed, so it's hard to tell who will win this . . ."

Michella counted the players on the bench that had been knocked out of the game. Both teams' Distracters were out, Linktie had three Fighters out and Ogragon had two. Cheers erupted from the stands followed by boos from the Ogragons as Michella looked up to see her brother Warren falling and a boy named Alan Fair looking down at him.

Ms Macay blew the whistle and Emily flew forward. She was the last hope for Ogragon to win. She looked at Alan and gulped. He was a hefty boy with short dark hair and a dimple in his chin. He cracked his knuckles with resentment and smirked at Emily. Emily stared back expressionless, even though the butterflies were whizzing around in her stomach.

The whistle blew and Alan flew towards Emily, who swiftly moved out of his grasp. He lunged at her again, trying desperately to grab her but Emily was too fast. Alan gritted his teeth, looking at Emily with frustration. Emily noticed he was wheezing slightly.

From the corner of her eye, Emily saw someone move near the commentators' box. She looked up and saw a muscular boy with a gaunt face and long, curly black hair standing on top of the commentators' box staring at her. She gasped when she recognised Lox and watched as he held up three fingers.

"What?" Emily shouted, hoping that he would read her lips, as her voice was drowned out by the gusty wind and the noisy crowd.

Lox pointed at each of his three fingers and pointed at Emily before he teleported. Emily looked wildly around but she couldn't see him. She turned around to see Alan reach for her again but this time Emily was too slow and he grabbed her tight around her small waist. He twisted her left arm with his rough, strong hands until Emily's screams rattled the invisible walls protecting the audience.

"Fair releases Knight but that arm must be in agony," Harmony Loving-Dale announced. "Fair throws a punch at her but misses by a long shot - glad to know that Knight realises that speed can be more useful than power - Knight's gone for a headlock but Fair's reversed it - into a bear hug! What is up with everyone using their bear hugs on her?"

"Too much for you, Knight?" Alan whispered into her ear.

Emily's head was throbbing. Her arm was sore and breathing in made her chest hurt. She was limp in Alan's arms for what seemed like hours, and she didn't even realise that that he had released her. She wouldn't have noticed that she was falling if the Ogragons weren't shouting at her to stop and banging on the invisible walls. Emily pulled her head up and managed to stop herself just before she touched the sandy pitch. She swayed from side to side trying to find her balance. She focused on Alan and began to fire Baby Balls at him as she flew up to his height, which he dodged effortlessly. She was out of breath when she reached him.

"Knight's energy seems to be running out - Fair's given her a jaw breaking punch which has sent Knight flying and what's this?" Wesley leaned forward in his seat. "Is he doing? Oh, no - Knight's in trouble now. Come on, Emily!"

Alan's punch had made Emily fly all the way to the other side of the stadium, where she painfully banged her back on the invisible wall. She looked up when she heard Wesley shout her name to see a blue fireball soaring towards her.

The fireball was close and Emily didn't have enough energy to move. She covered her face with her arms, hoping that the fireball would bounce off her like she had seen Master Zen demonstrate so many times in class but it didn't work. Emily's arms began to burn so she moved them and the fireball landed on her stomach. A strong, painful heat spread throughout her body. Emily screamed as her body was licked by the flames and the power of the fireball dragged her down on to the hard, sandy ground with an agonising thump.

A whistle blew faintly in Emily's ear. She could hear distant clapping and a hand placed itself under Emily's head, gently lifting her up. Someone poured Reviving Water into Emily's mouth which sent a comforting tingle down her body. She instantly felt energized and the pain had gone. Emily opened her eyes to see Wesley, Michella and Jason in front of her. The boys pulled her up by her arms to her feet.

"Don't tell me they won?"

"Yep," Jason said, watching the Linktie Dojo team hug Alan Fair. "That Alan dude must have been tough to take out you and Warren."

"Yeah, he was," Emily muttered, wiping the sand off her training kit.

"Let's get off the pitch before the Linkties come on," Wesley said.

Emily looked at the exits near the stands where the teachers were trying their hardest to control the rowdy crowd. The four of them hurried off the pitch and headed towards the changing room. It began to lightly drizzle.

"I won't be long. I'll meet you lot upstairs," Emily said.

They didn't argue with her as the rain fell hard. Emily watched them scurry across the damp floor before she entered the changing room. To her surprise, everyone was silent. She at least expected Lenny to be shouting the odds at them but he was folding up his Dojo kit, avoiding everyone's eye. They looked up as Emily entered and looked back down. Still nobody spoke so Emily didn't utter a word.

The rain had partnered up with the hailstones and they were coming down aggressively when Emily left the changing room. She didn't have a hood or umbrella so her hair got soaked instantly and a strong wind blew it in her face.

"Just great," Emily muttered. She brushed her hair back and wiped her damp face with her sleeve.

She walked through Gilford's Walk. She couldn't believe they were out of the running for the cup, that it was all over.

"Why did it have to be to Linktie?" she cried aloud.

Emily stopped. There was a strong presence surrounding her.

"Hello?" Emily shouted. She looked around but she could see nothing but the trees.

Something dark moved past her so fast, that by the time Emily turned around, it was already gone. A piece of paper was stuck to the tree next to her. Emily looked around but she could sense she was alone. Cautiously, Emily took of the piece of paper. She folded it up and sprinted towards the school. She couldn't hear footsteps behind her or sense anything but she wasn't taking any chances.

When she was safe in the corridor of Osaki, she kneeled over with her hands on her knees and took in deep sharp breaths. Students passed by and glanced at her curiously. She must have looked a mess with her damp hair stuck to her face but no one asked her anything. Emily sat at the bottom of the stairs, holding the side of her stomach until the stitch went away. She unfolded the piece of paper and began to read.

I AM...

Emily
Wait for three knocks on the Ogragon window at midnight.
Then meet me where we first spoke.
L

"You took your time," Jason said. He walked down the stairs, unaware of the two pretty blondes behind him, eyeing him up.

"Oh, sorry," Emily said, slipping the note into her pocket. "Is it time for dinner?"

"Yeah, Wesley and Michella have saved us seats, come on."

He linked arms with her and they walked into the dining hall together. Emily looked at the grandfather clock beside the dining room door. Only five hours till midnight.

CHAPTER ELEVEN

Midnight

Emily gulped down the bottle of Reviving Water. She threw it on the floor and charged at Wesley, who ducked under her legs and kicked her in her lower back. Emily spun around and fired a blue fireball at him. He flew above it and fired back a yellow fireball which Emily caught in her hands.

"I got it! I got it!" she said excitedly, as the class applauded her.

Emily shot the fireball into the Masonka wall which heaved forward as if it was taking in a deep breath and it swallowed up the fireball. Emily landed on the floor and punched the air.

"Did it hurt?" Daisy Atam asked.

"No, not at all!" Emily replied.

"Well done, Miss Knight," Master Zen said bowing to her and she bowed back.

"Mr Parker, why did you not catch the fireball?" Master Zen asked Wesley, who collapsed on the floor.

"Oh, it came too fast!" Wesley protested. He wiped his brow. "Next time, I'll get it."

"Good," Master Zen said. He threw a bottle of Reviving Water at Wesley who caught it and drank it down. "You're up against Miss Appleton."

"Oh come on sir!" Wesley said, sitting up. "I've done this four times in a row!"

"I could mark you down as a fail Mr Parker or you can go again."

Wesley rolled his eyes.

"This is a stupid exam," he muttered.

"Exams should be taken seriously. I'm being more than generous," Master Zen announced. "There is no reason for any of you to fail unless you are like Mr Parker who refuses to keep trying."

"I am trying," Wesley muttered under his breath. "It's hard."

"And this is why we try again," Master Zen smiled. "Let's go."

As Emily watched Wesley and Ambria Appleton battle, it dawned on her that it had been a month since she had received the note from Lox. She had even rented a room at Osaki, after convincing Sally and Michael that it would be easier for her to keep on top of her school work as everything she needed was there. Lucky for her, Michella's room had a spare bed and every night at midnight, Emily would wait for Lox's three knocks. She wasn't even sure what window he meant but so far she hadn't heard anything. She prayed that he was okay.

"Yes!" Wesley screamed as he held Ambria's pink fireball in the air like a trophy.

Emily applauded with the rest of the class but she couldn't clear her mind of Lox.

Even in Meditation class, Emily would usually lose her train of thought as she gazed at the stunning koi pond. She tried to focus on her breathing and stretching but Lox's face kept appearing in front of her.

"That was great!" Michella declared, as she stretched her arms up. "Much needed."

"Tell me about it," Jason said. "I'm loving the fact there are no exams for this lesson."

"No talk of exams please," Wesley stressed. "I can't wait till it's officially done with. I'm already over it."

The next week was devoted to revising and practising for Flying, Water Studies and History. Michella had made flash cards for the four of them and every evening before dinner, she would bombard them with questions and record their progress. So far, Jason was in the lead. Emily's head hurt from all the revision and her body ached from training but without fail she was awake till half past twelve waiting for Lox until she fell asleep.

Dojo practise had been suspended until the exams were over and every student was walking around the school in a zombie-like state, quoting passages to themselves. Tanya Frank was the only student who seemed to find the time to bother Emily about Ogragons' defeat to Linktie.

Whilst Emily was walking to her History exam, she got so frustrated with Tanya that she threw her History book at her when they passed each other in the hallway. Tanya fell to the floor, pretending that she had been knocked in the stomach by it.

"It's not that thick!" Emily protested to Ms Macay. "And it was her leg I threw it at."

"Detention with me on Friday," Ms Macay said, whilst a smirking Tanya stood behind her. "While everyone else is celebrating the end of exams, you will be with me in my office."

Emily stormed towards the dining hall, where the exams would be taking place. Michella, Wesley and Jason were huddled in the corner amongst stressed-out first years.

"Can you believe we only have twenty minutes to catch up on a year's worth of History?" Wesley said to Emily, as she re-opened her History book. "I'm kind of wishing now that Mr King had actually taught us more than what was the hot piece for the autumn/winter collection."

"Yeah, we're going to fail," Jason said, throwing his book to the side. "Why bother?"

I AM . . .

"You won't fail," Emily said, flicking through the book. "You can pass with your eyes closed unlike the rest of us."

"Positive energy guys, positive energy," Michella said, through gritted teeth.

They sat in silence until the teachers called them into the dining hall. Emily found her name near the middle of the hall and sat down.

"You have two hours to complete the paper. Begin," an examiner with a bald head said.

Emily looked around the hall at all the students writing. She closed her eyes briefly. *If you're real please help me pass* she prayed before she picked up her pen and began to write.

The air was humid and Emily pulled up the legs of her school training kit, so they hung like shorts. She couldn't wait till she could make a big bonfire to throw all her school books into.

"That was horrible," Wesley groaned, as they walked into the courtyard.

"It wasn't that bad," Michella said, in a cheery voice and Jason nodded in agreement.

Emily and Wesley stopped and pulled a face at them.

"Oh come on guys," Michella said, ignoring their angry faces. "Emily, what did you write for 2b?"

"Michella, please," Emily said, sitting on the grass. "Let's not re-live the torture."

"Oh, okay," Michella said, looking crestfallen until she started to wave her arms excitedly. "Julian! Julian, over here!"

"Must you call him over?" Wesley asked irritably. He kicked the stone in front of him. Emily ran a quick hand through her un-brushed hair and smiled as Julian approached them.

"Hey guys! How did you find it?" Julian asked.

"Great!" Michella said, before anyone else could speak. "Wasn't 2b easy? Obviously Mario Solis was the first warrior to ever get his powers."

Julian shook his head, "No, it was Edward Avard who got his powers first. Mario Solis was the youngest warrior to ever get his powers."

There was a brief silence where Emily looked from Michella to Julian. Wesley stifled his laughter.

"What?" Michella shouted. "I got it wrong? That was 40 marks!"

"I'm sorry," Julian said uncertainly, stepping back when he saw tears fall down Michella's cheeks.

"I revised so hard!" she cried.

"Oh, Mich, it's alright," Jason said, as he embraced her but she pushed him away.

"You wouldn't understand Jason! You knew it was Edward Avard." Michella narrowed her eyes accusingly at him.

"N-n-no I didn't," Jason lied.

"I'm never good at anything," Michella said, putting her head in her hands and Jason patted her back cautiously, in case she got angry again.

"Err . . . I think I'm going to head off now," Julian said.

He waved goodbye to Emily and half ran, half walked away from them, looking back as he went.

"Edward or Mario?" Wesley whispered to Emily.

"Edward," Emily said. "I guess God is real. You?"

"Charlie Simmons," Wesley replied. "So don't worry Michella, I failed too!"

"Shut up, Wesley," Michella snapped at him.

For the rest of the week, Michella refused to speak to Wesley because he was the most insensitive human being she had ever met.

Emily collapsed on to the couch in the living room, with a smile on her face. Exams were finally over. She was certain she had passed Flying.

I AM . . .

The circuit they had to fly around in under ten seconds was easy but Water Studies was in a league of its own. She was still unable to breathe under water and she was sure Mr Waternham had placed a big fat zero next to her name.

"Party tonight!" Warren Kinkle declared, as he walked into the living room, to cheers from fellow students.

"You going to let your hair down tonight, Ems?" Pete asked her, as he sat on the arm of the couch.

"Can't," Emily said bitterly. "Got detention with Ms Macay tonight. I want to kill that Tanya!"

"Aah, that's not cool. Me and Warren were thinking of inviting the other dorms in but obviously not the Linktie Dojo team. Got to get rid of potty-mouth Peterson, he'll be the first to run to Mr Davon."

"Well have fun," Emily sulked.

Pete ruffled her un-washed hair and Emily swatted his hand away. She glanced at the clock above her chair. Detention started in three hours.

Emily sat at the dining table next to an excited Wesley, who was rubbing his hands at the sight of the piping hot bowls of apple crumble and vanilla ice-cream. Emily clapped her hands and licked her lips. She lifted up her spoon and scooped up a big piece of apple crumble when she felt a hand rest heavily on her shoulder.

"Come on Knight, time for detention," Ms Macay said, staring at her over her glasses.

Emily's mouth dropped, "Are you serious? I haven't even had desert!"

Ms Macay shrugged her thin shoulders, "That's life. Come now, let's not waste time."

Emily sighed heavily and dropped her spoon into her desert bowl. Wesley lunged for it and Michella looked at him in disgust.

"For goodness sake, wait till she's left the table!"

Wesely blushed and removed his hands from the bowl, "Sorry."

Emily dragged her feet behind Ms Macay. Tanya waved at her as she walked out but Emily ignored her. She wasn't taking any chances with Ms Macay.

Ms Macay's office was next to the Ogragon bedrooms. It was a cosy office with pictures of famous warriors plastered across the walls. Two beige armchairs were facing each other next to the roaring fireplace. Ms Macay sat in one of the armchairs, Emily went to sit in the other when Ms Macay glared at her.

"This is a detention Miss Knight not a girly chat. Go and sit at the table in the corner."

Emily followed Ms Macay's gaze and stared at the small, white table, far away from the heat of the fireplace. Emily sat on it and picked up the sheets of paper on the table.

"What's this?" she asked Ms Macay, who smirked.

"Your work for tonight. I want you to write me an essay on the fundamentals of flying. There are quotes on the sheets of paper that I would like you to include. Make it good Knight!"

Emily sighed. She watched Ms Macay lean back in her big armchair and pick up a book with a man and a woman running along a beach. Ms Macay caught her watching.

"Begin now!"

Emily quickly turned around, leaned over and began to write.

Several hours had gone by and Emily's wrist was hurting. She was only halfway through the essay because it took so long to find the right quote. Ms Macay was engrossed in her book and Emily had a feeling that she had forgotten that she was still there. A loud drum beat vibrated through out the room and laughter echoed down the corridor. Ms Macay looked around the room.

"Where is that noise coming from?"

Emily glanced at her watch. It was coming to midnight and it sounded like Warren and Pete's party was in full swing.

I AM ...

"Knight, I'll be right back," Ms Macay said. She slipped on her high heels and marched out of the door.

As soon as the door had shut, Emily heard three taps on the window. She looked over but nobody was there. She ran over to the window and looked down but it was so dark, she couldn't see anything. She opened the window and leaned out.

"Lox?" Emily called but no one replied.

Ms Macay walked back into the room.

"Knight, what are you doing?" she snapped.

"Oh, I thought I heard something outside," Emily said, closing the window.

Ms Macay shook her head and kicked off her high heels.

"It's probably kids celebrating the end of exams. Can you believe that just down the hall, there was a party with drinks and everything?"

"No way," Emily said in mock disbelief.

Ms Macay looked at her watch and gasped, "Wow, is that the time? I think it's bedtime for you young lady."

"Oh, great!" Emily said running towards the door.

"Emily."

Emily turned around.

"A piece of advice. Stop letting Miss Frank get to you. Is it really worth it?"

"No Miss," Emily replied.

Ms Macay smiled at her, "You're a good kid, go on."

Emily smiled and sprinted down the corridor to her bedroom. She could still hear students talking in the living room. Emily hoped that her room was empty. She opened the door and no one was there. Emily ran to her closet and rummaged through it, throwing clothes on to the floor until she found her blue jumper and jeans. She hurriedly put them on and kicked off her baht shoes, replacing them with scuffed trainers.

The door opened and a giggling Violet Hijen stood in the doorway, holding hands with a mixed race boy. He whispered in her ear and she playfully hit him.

"Stop," Violet flirted. "What do you want to do? We're all alone now."

"No you're not!" Emily said horrified.

"Oops," Violet giggled, closing the door. "Your room it is."

Emily ran across the room and threw open the bedroom door. A swaying Michella fell heavily into her arms.

"Oh, Emily. I am glad to see you," Michella said, before she hunched over and collapsed into a fit of laughter.

"Are you drunk?" Emily asked amazed, as she studied Michella's glazed eyes.

"Am I ever!" Michella shouted.

She placed her hands on Emily's shoulders and pulled herself up. She stared intensely into Emily's eyes.

"I love you," she slurred. "From this wall."

Michella ran to one side of the room, "To that one."

She ran towards the other side of the room but she tripped over Emily's baht shoes. Michella fell on to her knees, threw her head back and laughed. Emily grabbed her waist and walked her slowly to her bed. Michella threw herself on to the bed and grabbed hold of Emily's neck so she fell on top of her.

"I love having you live here. You're like the sister I never had."

"Michella," Emily cried irritably, wrenching Michella's hands from around her neck. "You have two sisters and I've got to go."

"Where?" Michella asked frowning.

"To meet someone."

"Who?"

Emily looked at Michella. She was sounding like her old self. Her eyes were alert and suspicious and she no longer slurred her words.

"Just a friend," Emily replied.

"Well, I'm coming with you," Michella said, sitting up.

"We're going for a walk outside. You need some sleep."

"Outside?" Michella smiled. "Great, I need some fresh air."

"No!" Emily cried desperately, making Michella jump. "I just need to go by myself."

Michella swayed as she stood up and faced Emily.

"I may be a little drunk but I'm not stupid Emily," Michella said, burping loudly. "Where are you going? And your little hints are giving me a headache."

Emily wanted to point out that the alcohol was obviously giving her a headache but Michella was looking at her sternly.

Emily sighed heavily, "Lox."

"What?" Michella frowned.

"Lox. I'm going to meet Lox."

Michella stared at Emily baffled. "Lox? As in your brother?"

Emily nodded.

Michella shook her dazed head and fell back on to the bed, "But how? I mean, when did you find him?"

"The day when me, you and Jason were on Gilford's Walk. Remember that power we felt?"

"It was so strong," Michella said, looking up at her.

"Well, it was Lox. Something isn't right with him Michella. I think he's in some kind of trouble."

"What makes you think that?" Michella asked.

"He was so scared that someone would hear us. Some girl. I don't know who he was talking about but he looked so distressed and he kept telling me to choose, saying that it wasn't safe for me but I didn't know what he meant. I got a note from him after the Linktie match, asking me to meet him. Maybe he'll tell me what's going on."

Michella shook her head slowly, "There's something funny about this. Why didn't he just tell you what's going on? Did he explain where he ran away to?"

Emily shook her head.

"Emily, I don't think you should go," Michella said. "Something doesn't feel right."

"What?" Emily yelled. "He's my brother!"

"I know," Michella said, standing up and gripping Emily's arm because she was swaying again. "But you don't even know him. Not really. I just have a bad feeling about this."

"You don't know him," Emily said fiercely. "I'm going."

"Fine," Michella said, shrugging her shoulders. "I'll just have to come with you."

"Michella, you're drunk," Emily spat impatiently.

"And you're hard headed. Now, where's my other shoe?"

Michella pointed down to her vibrant pink sock.

Emily looked at her watch. It was twenty past midnight.

It took a further ten minutes for them to find Michella's missing shoe. It was at the bottom of the toilet.

"What kind of party was this?" Emily asked, as a disgusted Michella fished out her shoe.

"I can't really remember," Michella replied truthfully.

When Michella had put on a clean, dry pair of shoes, they ran into the living room. Wesley and Jason were sitting on the armchairs beside the fire place. The living room was a mess. There was food and empty bottles everywhere. The four of them looked at each other in surprise.

"Hey, Michella," Jason said smiling and Michella looked away embarrassed.

"The party's moved to the Pentwon room," Wesley said. He sat up in his seat as he looked at Emily's attire. "You're not dressed for a party, Emily?"

"Where are you two going at half twelve?" Jason asked, glancing at his watch.

"We're going to meet someone but it's a secret," Michella said and just in case they didn't get the message, she held up a finger to her lips and said "Ssh."

Emily rolled her eyes, "Come on."

Emily led the way, hurriedly running down the steps. The school was unusually quiet and Cecil and Niles weren't floating around the corridors, so they managed to leave the building unnoticed.

"Where are we going?" Wesley asked, jogging up to Emily.

"Why are you here?" Emily snapped. "Go back."

"We're going to meet Lox," Michella shouted.

"Your brother?" Jason called from behind her.

"Keep it down," Emily barked. "I don't want you lot to scare him away."

They scurried through the dark forest. Branches whipped the side of Emily's arms and behind her, Michella buckled over a log. Emily kept going until she saw the spot where she first saw Lox. It was empty.

"Stay here," Emily instructed.

"No way," Michella replied, before she collapsed on to the grassy floor.

"Is she alright?" Wesley asked Emily.

"I'm dizzy," Michella said, from the ground.

"Keep an eye on her, I won't be long."

Emily walked with her head down to avoid hitting the sharp twigs. A light was shining bright at the spot she stood at previous months before. She looked up, smiling at the full moon.

"Lox," Emily called softly.

She closed her eyes in an attempt to sense him but she felt nothing.

"YOU'RE DRUNK!" Wesley hollered. "ARE YOU STUPID?"

Emily jumped.

"WHAT THE HELL IS WRONG WITH YOU? YOU THINK IT'S FUN TO DRINK?"

"I-I-I-I wasn't thinking," Michella sobbed. "Ah man, my head hurts. Wesley, please don't be angry."

"Good I'm glad it hurts, you stupid girl!" Wesley shouted.

Emily heard Jason intervene, talking softly so she couldn't hear. Emily looked around one last time but Lox wasn't there. She sighed and turned to walk back into the bushes.

A strong arm grabbed her around the waist and a rough hand covered her mouth.

"Don't move," a voice whispered menacingly into her ear and before she knew it, Emily was soaring high into the air, her terrified eyes darting to and fro.

CHAPTER TWELVE

Lox's Story

Emily was flying so fast that the wind was hitting her face, making her eyes water. Emily tried to turn her head but a sharp pain hit her in her lower back. Emily looked down, staring at the stadium. It had been swallowed up by the darkness but she could make out the commentators' box. They soared past it quickly. Emily looked straight ahead. They were heading towards the mountain.

Unexpectedly, the person holding her dived, making her stomach feel like it was trying to escape through her throat. Emily's muffled screams rang in her ears. They landed gracefully on the muddy floor. They were deep inside the forest. The person spun Emily around and she looked into the eyes of her brother, Lox. His brown eyes stared coldly at her.

"What the hell are you doing?" Emily screamed, pushing him hard.

Lox wobbled slightly and smiled, "Sorry, did I scare you?"

"Did you think that was funny? Kidnapping your own sister."

"I didn't kidnap you Emily," Lox said, rolling his eyes. "Don't be so dramatic."

"And do you have any idea, how many windows there are in the Ogragon room?"

Lox laughed, "My bad. I wrote it vague in case anyone found the letter. Sorry."

He placed a pocket knife from his hand into his trouser pocket. He caught Emily looking at it.

"It's for protection," he explained.

"From who?"

"Everyone."

"Why, when you have powers?" Emily asked.

"This is more discreet than shooting fireballs."

Lox sat down on the edge of a rock, "So, I thought I said to be alone."

"I have persistent friends," Emily said, sitting on the rock opposite him. "Is that why you brought me here?"

Lox nodded, "A bit of privacy with my baby sister, that's all I wanted."

They sat in silence. Lox tapped his worn out trainers on the grassy floor. Emily stared at his gaunt face. Lox flicked his long, dark hair out of his face and looked up at Emily.

"I saw your Dojo match. You fight well. Almost as good as me," Lox laughed.

"Oh, thanks," Emily said uncertainly, remembering how Alan Fair had defeated her.

"We can definitely use your skills."

Emily frowned, "Who's we?"

Lox stood up and began to pace. Emily watched him anxiously.

"Remember I said you had to choose?"

Emily nodded.

"Well . . . have you picked?" Lox asked hopefully.

Emily laughed, "You still haven't told me what my choices are."

Lox stopped pacing. His face was hard, "This is not a laughing matter Emily. A lot is at stake here."

I AM . . .

Emily shifted uncomfortably on the rock, "Like what?"

"I've been reading about you, making the papers all the time," Lox said, ignoring her question. "Don't you think it's funny how people's opinions can change when they need something? First you're in the paper for stealing and now it's to be our new hero, here to save us all."

Lox laughed to himself.

"Just like our Daddy," he finished bitterly.

Emily frowned, "Didn't you think our Dad was a hero?"

"Oh, Emily," Lox said, his voice rising. "You really have no clue."

"So why don't you enlighten me?" Emily asked, frustrated.

A flash of anger went through Lox's eyes, "Our Dad. The great Thomas Knight, was a selfish, arrogant git who didn't care about me, you or Mum."

Emily shook her head, "That's not true."

"Really?" Lox said, eyes wide. "When was the last time he came to visit you? You were so young, you didn't even know that he wasn't around. He was out flying all over the world playing the 'hero' and I had to look after you and Mum. I had to deal with all the rumours."

Emily stood up, "What rumours?"

Lox laughed bitterly again, "The ones about him and Roberta. That was the main one, although I'm sure there were more women."

"That's a lie!" Emily shouted.

Lox shrugged his shoulders, "Believe what you want about him but I know the truth. Did you know I was six when Dad entered me into battles? Media hype everywhere, pressure like you wouldn't believe because I was Thomas Knight's son. I looked like him, I walked like him, I even fought like him. I won every battle he made me enter and every picture I have, he's there. Standing next to me like the proud father, taking credit for all of my hard work."

Lox stood up and began to march up and down with his fist clenched, "But no one took notice of the other side. How he was never around. How his wife was dying of cancer yet he was too busy to support her. I was nine and I was left to look after you and our dying mum, while our dad pranced around the place like he was some King!"

Lox stared into space breathing heavily. Emily shook her head in disbelief.

"Why are you telling me this?"

"Because it's the truth," Lox spat. "You were lucky."

"I was lucky?" Emily asked, walking up towards him. "I had to learn about my family from a text book or the newspaper, so please someone tell me, how am I so lucky? Who the hell am I, Lox? I've learnt more about myself in this school, than I've known in my lifetime. My Mum died, my Dad is God knows where and my brother left me, all by myself. Now who's selfish?"

"Emily it wasn't -"

"No, Lox because from what I can remember, Dad left to go and find you!" She pointed accusingly at him. "Did you think I'd forgotten? It's in my head all the time, it's even in my dreams. I remember you two arguing and you storming upstairs, blaring your music really loud. Mum was so upset."

Emily wiped her wet face with her top, "The whole world knows that Thomas Knight won't return until he has you home safe and sound and guess what Lox? He still isn't back because he's still looking for you. So if anyone has the right to be angry here it's me! I'm not angry at him Lox. So the same day you try to make me turn against my own father will be the same day I turn against you. Don't. Push. Me."

The pair stared at each other, their chests rising and falling rapidly. Lox put his hands up as if he was surrendering, "Okay, I won't say anymore."

Lox sat back on the edge of the rock. He tapped his battered trainers on the ground and glanced at his watch. Emily took in a deep breath and exhaled. She could feel her anger level dropping.

I AM . . .

"Why did you leave?"

Lox stayed quiet and Emily feared he wouldn't answer.

"I just had enough," he said softly. "I just couldn't take it anymore. I just wanted him to notice me. Not as his protégé but as me. Just his son. I wasn't planning to go for long, I just wanted to scare him. There was an underground spot I was going to stay at for a while but that night, I met someone."

"Who?"

"A lady," Lox said, looking at her. "She knew all about me and Dad's relationship. She never told me how she knew but she knew a lot. She saw what I saw in him and she wanted to take me under her wing and train me up. She hated him even more than I did. I didn't realise who it was . . . but I eventually did . . ."

Lox hung his head and Emily watched as his shoulders shook and he whimpered softly. She ran to him and held him tight. His tears splashed on to her face.

"What happened Lox?"

"I - I did s-something so stupid," he stammered.

"What did you do? Tell me Lox!" she yelled.

"Neci," he whispered.

Emily jumped back as if she had been burnt. If there was a warrior to be scared of it was Neci but Thomas Knight had defeated her in one of warrior history's best battles. She looked at Lox. She was waiting for him to laugh and say he was joking but he was staring at the floor.

"Neci left after she murdered Cecil and Niles. Dad defeated her, everyone knows that."

Lox shook his head and Emily fell quiet.

"She was the lady who came to me. I swear Emily, I didn't know it was her at first. She was wearing this mask but when I found out, I had no choice."

"No choice about what?" Emily whispered, torn between listening and running away form Lox's confession.

"To join her army," Lox looked up at her. He was shaking. "You know Neci came at the height of the Five Warriors' fame? Well, she quickly gained a reputation for beating the strongest warriors, winning championships and killing her opponents. It was actually her who challenged Dad and the others to a battle. She was so confident she could beat these over-hyped teenagers. I remember Dad telling me about the battle and how heartbroken he was when she killed Cecil and Niles. Dad said that was the first time he had ever wanted to kill someone."

Lox picked at the hole in his bottoms, "But he didn't because Dad could never do that. He said it would have made him just like her so he let her live and she teleported. Dad was now an even bigger celebrity, everyone felt safe and Neci was finally gone. The problem was she didn't just disappear. She was really pissed off."

"So what happened?" Emily asked. She noticed how Lox looked again at his watch.

"She wanted revenge. Neci's whole being is to be number one. She wants to run the world. She wants to eliminate all the warriors that are against her or pose a threat. She knew Dad was too strong for her so she began to recruit powerful, unique warriors to take down Dad. An army. And that's where you come in."

Lox stood up and stared hard at Emily, "What side are you on?"

"Whoa, hold on a minute," Emily said, taking a step back. "You want me to pick between Dad and Neci? Are you insane?"

"This is not a joke, Emily."

Lox glanced again at his watch.

"And what's with the watch? Are you late for something?"

"We don't have a lot of time. Pick a side." Lox stressed.

"I will not pick Neci!"

"You have to!" Lox yelled.

"Why?"

"Because she'll kill you!"

Emily shook her head slowly, "Lox this is crazy, why would she?"

Lox looked up at the dark sky, "Because you're a Knight, Ems. Because you're strong and that makes you a threat. I'm not a threat anymore. I picked my side a long time ago but you are. That's why I'm here to take you home."

"I have a home Lox!" Emily cried outraged. "I would never pick Neci. Never! How did you even know . . ."

Emily stopped and remembered the boy at Lox's bedroom window with the huge power. Emily stared at Lox as if seeing him for the first time.

"It was you wasn't it? At your bedroom at the house?"

Lox nodded, "I had to see you before you came here."

"WHY!" Emily screamed in his face.

"This is my assignment Emily, to get you!"

Emily gasped, "No . . . no you're lying."

"My task was to get you on board but when I first saw you, you didn't agree to go with me. Neci wasn't happy and she told me to kill you. So I came to your Revolution Night party and broke into your friend's house. I can sense your power anywhere but each time, I couldn't do it. I could have teleported you anytime, killed you with a single fireball but I couldn't. I couldn't because you're my baby sister."

"So what are we doing here Lox?" Emily asked. Tears were falling fast down her face. "Let me go back."

Lox shook his head. A tear raced from his eyes down to the edge of his chin, where it fell, "They're coming. The others are coming."

"What?" Emily looked around wildly, wishing she could see her surroundings but it was too dark.

He suddenly grabbed Emily's hands and squeezed them tight, looking at her urgently, "Emily, you need to go. You need to go now, there's a bit of ti -"

Lox's eyes rolled to the back of his head and he fell heavily into Emily's arms. Emily screamed and hurriedly placed him on the floor. She squinted in the dark in front of her. She couldn't see anything. She took off her jumper and put it under Lox's head and wiped his hair off his face. His eyes were closed, he wasn't moving but he was breathing.

Emily stood up and caught her breath. There were four warriors dressed in black surrounding her and Lox. They covered every corner so Emily couldn't escape. The one on her left was an eerily beautiful, red headed woman with full, red lips and green, mesmerizing eyes, standing silent and tall. To her right was a gangly woman with short, brown, curly hair and frog like eyes. Emily looked behind her and a short, black man with a black mohican smiled at her. His gold, front tooth glistened. The one in front of Emily made her feel cold inside. Her face was hidden behind a white mask and her power energy was so strong, that it felt like it was surrounding her. It was Neci.

"Finally we meet," Neci said softly. "Well done, Lox."

Emily glanced at Lox, he was still. Her breathing felt loud in her ears and her voice shook when she asked, "W-well done f-for what? He failed your task, he didn't kill me."

Neci chuckled, "I'm sure you realise by now, young Knight, that this was a set up? Lox planned this arrangement perfectly. Because family, yours in particular, always look out for number one."

A cracking noise came from behind her. Emily saw the man with the mohican, stretching out his neck from side to side. When he saw Emily watching, he grinned and winked at her. Emily turned back around.

"Your power energy is breathtaking," Neci said slowly. "It's a shame."

Neci shot a red fireball that flew rapidly at Emily and hit her hard in her stomach. She toppled backwards and rolled on the floor screaming, holding her stomach tight as the pain soared through her body.

"What are you doing?" Emily cried, as she withered in pain.

"Get up," Neci said sharply.

Emily looked at Lox. If only she could reach him, she knew it would be all right. She didn't know how she knew but if she could touch him, she could get them back to the school but he was too far away.

"Ladies, let's show Knight what we do with people who don't listen."

The red head and the curly haired woman opened their fists and shot two yellow fireballs at Emily. Emily reached out her hands and caught one of the yellow fireballs. It was burning her hands but Emily gritted her teeth and turned her torso, to catch the other one. The yellow fireballs merged into one and Emily shot it at Neci. Neci swatted it away, like it was an annoying fly and the fireball flew into the forest. Emily groaned and fell on to her knees as sweat trickled down her forehead. Her stomach was in too much pain to support her.

"Not bad," Neci said. "Take them both!"

The three warriors marched towards Emily.

"I'm not dying, I'm not dying," Emily chanted to herself.

The mohican man grabbed her leg roughly and Emily kicked him with her other leg, so he stumbled back.

"Bless her," the curly haired lady mocked.

She grabbed both of Emily's legs and pulled her hard so Emily fell on to her sore stomach. Sharp pains shot through her body.

"LEAVE ME ALONE!"

Emily saw their shocked faces before the forest was covered in a blinding white light. Emily's legs were released and she could hear the warriors screaming. Emily tried to open her eyes but the bright light made it impossible to. She kept them shut and stretched her arms out in front of her. Her fingers felt through the grass and dirt before she caught hold of Lox's toned torso. Emily gripped it tight and shut her eyes.

Neci stumbled in the bright light. She couldn't see Emily and Lox. She reached out desperately to where Emily had been but Emily and Lox were gone.

Mr Davon was standing by the window in his office. His hands were clasped behind his back and his eyes were fixated on the blinding light that had covered the forest. He spun around to see Emily and Lox appear on the floor of his office. Emily collapsed on top of Lox, breathing hard and fast. Mr Davon ran around his office table and knelt by Emily.

"Neci, she's here," Emily whispered painfully.

Mr Davon nodded and a second later, all of the school's teachers had appeared in the office. They gasped as they saw Emily, dirty and scarred on top of a motionless Lox.

"Is that -" Cecil began but Mr Davon silenced him.

"Check the entire building, the forest, all of our grounds and make sure that Neci and her henchmen are gone."

The teachers nodded and teleported from the office. Nurse Hilda was the only one to stay behind. Mr Davon tapped Emily lightly on the arm.

"Emily, we have to take you and Lox to the sick bay. I need you to get off him."

Emily shook her head and held on tighter to him, "I'm not letting go until he wakes up."

Mr Davon nodded at Nurse Hilda who removed her white surgical gloves.

"We will talk in the morning," Mr Davon said earnestly to Emily before Nurse Hilda put her cold hand on Emily's forehead and everything went black.

Emily slowly opened her eyes and looked down at the white gown she was wearing. She lifted it up and saw the bandages across her stomach.

I AM...

She touched it gently and flinched. The sick bay was quiet. Emily looked around at the cream walls, covered with paintings of warriors healing sick and injured people.

On her bedside table was a bouquet of sunflowers, cards and chocolates. Emily gritted her teeth, ignoring the pain as she reached for a card. It wasn't as pretty as the other cards, in fact it was written on a torn piece of paper. *Sorry x Lox*, the letter read. A panic stricken Emily turned to the right of her bed. The bed next to hers looked freshly slept in.

"No, no, no," Emily cried.

She tried to sit up but her stomach muscles still wouldn't support her and she fell back painfully on to the bed.

"Nurse Hilda! Nurse Hilda!"

A plump woman with a tight, blonde bun hurried towards Emily.

"Miss Knight what's wrong?"

"He's gone," Emily said. "We need to find him!"

Nurse Hilda glanced at the untidy bed and sighed, "I'm sorry Miss Knight but your brother is not a student at this school so we are under no obligation to find him."

"We need to get him back," Emily cried. "Please."

"I'm sorry," Nurse Hilda replied.

"Please, Nurse Hilda please! She'll hurt him!"

"Miss Knight, calm down or I'll have to put you to sleep!"

"I don't care. I'll go myself."

Emily closed her eyes tight, praying she'll get a sense of where he was. If she could only teleport like she did last night but before anything had a chance to happen, Nurse Hilda's cold hand hit her forehead, draining all of her power so Emily had no choice but to fall asleep.

It was a week later when Nurse Hilda permitted Emily to have guests. Mr Davon was the first one to visit and when he arrived, Emily had just finished reading the Daily Steward. There was still no news on Lox or Neci.

"How are you feeling?" Mr Davon asked. He sat at the side of Emily's bed.

"Okay," she replied, folding up the paper. "I had a dream that Neci murdered Lox. Will she? I mean, will she kill him?"

Mr Davon massaged his brow, "I don't know."

Emily sighed and muttered, "He didn't want to kill me."

"I know," Mr Davon said. "Emily, I spoke to Lox before he left."

"You did?" Emily asked, sitting up. "What happened? What did he say?"

"He told me that Neci's goal is to kill Thomas Knight and any other powerful warriors against her. I assume that apart from you that will include Roberta Taniana and Hubert Jenkins as the last remaining Five Warriors. He also said the task would begin once you came to Osaki because only here would you grow and become a threat. Lox said he tried to warn you not to come?"

Emily nodded. Now she realised he had meant that she shouldn't go to the school. He was trying to protect her. If only he had been clearer with his message. If only he had trusted her and told her what was going on.

"So has he gone back to her?"

Mr Davon shook his head, "He's gone into hiding."

Emily was quiet as she digested this. *Where would he go? Would I ever see him again?*

"Mr Davon?"

"Yes?" he said.

"You know that light that covered the forest. I think . . . I think it was from me."

I AM...

Mr Davon smiled, "It certainly was. Once again, it was your emotions controlling your power. I'm assuming they weren't particularly happy when that happened."

Emily painfully laughed, "No they weren't. It was weird you know, I didn't even try to make it happen. I've never been taught how to do a light beam."

"All the more reason why we need to get it under control."

"And I teleported too. I don't know how but I knew I could teleport us back to the school even though I'd never done it before."

Mr Davon stood up, "The sooner we get it under control the better."

Mr Davon was nearly at the door when Emily called to him.

"Sir, were my Dad and Roberta . . . I mean, did they ever have a relationship?"

Emily gripped the bed sheet tight.

"Emily, you of all people need to learn that fame comes at a price and if you don't create your own dirt, someone will do it for you. Countless rumours have been told about Thomas and Roberta's 'special relationship,' which I've never seen," and with that Mr Davon left the sick bay, leaving Emily alone.

It was two weeks after the talk with Mr Davon when Emily was completely healed and free to leave the sick bay. Sally and Michael were coming to pick her up later that evening so Emily spent the afternoon outside in the sun. She sat under the willow tree with Michella, Wesley and Jason.

"How busted was Tanya's nose?" Emily asked gleefully. "I can't believe I missed the Dojo finals!"

"Disgusting! It looks like a beach ball is stuck to her face" Michella responded. "Bet she's happy that we're going home this weekend."

"We have to win the cup next year, man," Jason said. "This is Pentwon's third year in a row and they're crap."

Emily laughed, "Don't worry we will."

Wesley picked up a daffodil by his foot and was picking off the petals one by one, "Emily, do you think your Dad knows about Lox?"

"Probably," Emily said, as she lay down on the grass. "I mean everyone knows he was near the school now because of the Daily Steward article this morning but Michael tried to call my Dad, to tell him about Lox but couldn't get through to him. Hopefully someone will. Hey -" Michella, Wesley and Jason looked at her, "You lot never even told me what happened when Lox flew me away."

"Well Miss party girl over here and loud mouth," Jason said, glancing at Michella and Wesley. "They were making so much noise that it took us ages to realise that you were gone and when we did, we obviously didn't have a clue. So we decided to go and tell Mr Davon but when we were nearly out of the forest, that yellow fireball came out of nowhere, nearly taking our heads off! Anyway, we thought it might have something to do with you, so we started to run back but you covered the forest with a light beam so it took us years to find our way out. When we did get to Mr Davon, he said you had already arrived."

Emily sat up, "I'm sorry guys for everything. I should have let you know about Lox from before."

"Don't worry, the most important thing is you're still here," Michella said, grabbing Emily's hand and squeezing it tight. "And that we passed our exams," Michella said as an afterthought.

A large group of students ran past them. Wesley looked at his watch and yelped.

"The match, the match."

The four of them got up and ran into the school and into the dining hall which was rammed with students, watching the biggest Dojo match of the year, England v Germany. Emily spotted Tanya in the corner with Fiona Corn and Ola Ade. She had a white bandage over her swollen, purple nose. Tanya looked over and saw Emily. She tried to cover her nose with her hand and Emily laughed.

"Go on Janette! That's it!" Warren yelled at the screen, as Janette Kinkle kicked a Germany Distracter hard on the shoulder.

"What's wrong with the TV?" Summer Wind asked.

The picture flickered back and forth and the colour had changed to black and white.

"I don't know," Mr King said, getting up and hitting the side of the TV.

"Do you think it's the signal?" a boy called from the back.

"Maybe," Mr King said, looking at it closely.

The screen turned pitch black and everyone groaned.

"I didn't touch it, I swear!" Mr King cried, jumping away from the TV.

The black screen began to flicker and then the screen was back again but it was not of Lordsway Stadium. It was of a tall, slender woman dressed in a black cloak and a white mask. Silence fell and an air of coldness seemed to hover in the room. The picture was unsteady as if someone was filming with a hand held camera and it was focused on one person in the middle. Neci.

"This isn't a time for forgiveness," she said softly. "Or a time for love and consolation."

"Turn it up!" someone said.

"Sssh," everyone said and Mr King turned up the volume.

"This is a time for power and alliances and for me to take back what is mine. I will claim back my title as the best warrior and any warrior that gets in my way will be killed. Once I get back my missing warrior, I will murder any warriors that support Thomas Knight, Roberta Taniana, Hubert Jenkins, Cecil Archinia and Niles Thompson. All those that betrayed me will feel my wrath when I find them.

"Come over to me if you want to be an immortal. I will show you true power, we welcome you with open hands. Those who resist will be at war with us, so pick a side and let the games begin."

The screen flickered again and the picture turned black. The hall was silent until someone from the front asked, "Was that a hoax? It was a hoax right?" and then everyone began to talk at once.

A strong power level came from behind Emily and she turned to find Mr Davon behind her. He grabbed hold of her shoulder and gently squeezed it. They caught each others eye and Emily nodded because she understood that if she wanted to live, this was a war she had to be ready for.

Lightning Source UK Ltd.
Milton Keynes UK
UKOW032348180912

199204UK00001B/18/P